# Strands Across the Sea

*Distance will not destroy the strands
that tie this family together*

**Copyright 2014
Helen Reardon**



ISBN 978-0-473-27443-6

# Strands across the Sea
## Prologue 1863

*The tall ship lurched as the white-crested waves tumbled into the normally calm bay.*
*The peaceful village of Tobermory on the island of Mull was about to witness a sight that would change the lives of many of its inhabitants forever.*

*Groups of people stood on the jetty and lined the seafront as a tender was rowed out to the ship carrying trunks and boxes, baskets and bundles, all bound for the colony of New Zealand.*

*Margaret McDonald fought back the tears that threatened to overwhelm her as she held her precious children for the last time. So many of her family were about to make the long journey to that far-off land. But she, the matriarch, had to remain strong.*

*Her husband Archibald stood by her side, staring bleakly out into the bay. He turned to the son who stood beside him and shook him by the hand. "I know you will make us proud. Look after each other and good luck to you in the new land."*

*And then it was time for the women and children to climb aboard the small craft which would take them out to the waiting ship. Some shed silent tears but others set up a wailing that echoed eerily around the hills.*

*Children cried as they were lifted onto the boats that rocked and swayed beside the jetty. The women clutched their skirts as they stepped down to join their bairns, many turning to wave to the assembled crowd until they were rowed far out on the bay.*

*Then it was the turn of the men folk to say their last farewells to family and friends and head off for the greatest adventure of their lives, a fresh start in New Zealand, the land of hope and opportunity.*

# Chapter 1

The notice in the window of the general store caught everybody's eye. The whole village was talking about it and when Donald McArthur wheeled his baskets of shoes along the cobbled street, he too, stopped to see what all the excitement was about.

"There's a ship to be sailing from Tobermory right across the world to far-off New Zealand." A stocky young man pulled a cap over his tousled hair and turned to face Donald. "And there'll be no more young ones left in the town before much longer. Just you mark my words."

Donald looked at the large piece of parchment with the thick black lettering. He could make out most of what was written but knew full well that many of those around him were not so lucky. "A new ship will sail right from this jetty in three months time," he read out to the gathered crowd. "There'll be space for 200, and families are encouraged to try their luck in the new colony."

He shook his head at the thought of travelling all those miles and spending many weeks on board a crowded ship. He had considered immigrating to Canada at one time when the offer was made, but what would his wife Chirsty say?

"New Zealand! Myself and the children won't be going there. That's about as far away as you can go."

Donald pulled his load further along the street until he came to the stone building where leather goods were sold. His strong working boots and soft slippers for the more privileged women were earning him a good reputation. Archie Black, the storekeeper was busy with a customer so Donald unloaded two baskets of shoes and boots onto the floor beside the wooden counter.

The storekeeper smiled a greeting and was soon checking out the quality of the new batch of footwear. "Aye, you have done a good job once again. These boots will sell well and if ever anyone has money to spend on fancy slippers I'm sure these will catch their eye."

"I see there's a ship sailing right out of Tobermory, bound for New Zealand." Donald was keen to share the news. "I feel it's too late for my family, what with four children already and Chirsty ready to produce another at any time."

Archie Black looked at Donald with a twinkle in his eye. "It's living on that desolate island that's doing it. You need to move into the village and life will be too busy to lie about in bed." He laughed. "But you are still determined to stay on Ulva, in spite of the best efforts of the owner to clear the land for sheep."

Donald looked solemn. "In truth, there are few of us left, and we are now all living on the God forsaken shore at Ardglass. If it wasn't for Chirsty's father being determined to live out his days there we'd be on the move tomorrow."

"You'd do well to settle in Tobermory where there is more chance to find work," advised the storekeeper. "You could set up repairing boots for those who can't afford a new pair."

Donald thanked his friend for his advice and set off back to the jetty to return the cart. The next boat to Ulva wasn't due for two hours so he decided to walk up the Back Brae to the Upper Village where rows of sturdy cottages were overflowing with the people who had been forced to move from the smaller islands.

He continued up to the very top of the hill until he reached the graveyard where fine Celtic crosses intermingled with simple stone markers. From here he could look out across Tobermory Bay where many boats were anchored in the calm waters. In the distance, a number of small islands merged with the hazy sea and grey clouds gathered overhead, for a moment shutting out the welcome spring sunshine.

He looked down towards the jetty where the ship would leave in a few short months, perhaps carrying away many of his friends. "New Zealand. What an adventure that would be." He spoke aloud. There was no-one in the graveyard to hear his words. "But it would be too long a journey for Chirsty and the bairns."

He sighed and headed back down the hill, past the women gossiping over the rock walls and the children playing in the dusty streets. With money in his pocket he had goods to buy at the store before heading back to his family on the island.

As the small craft pulled into the primitive landing back on Ulva, Donald gathered up his baskets which were now filled with produce from the store in Tobermory. Archie Black had paid him well for the last batch of shoes and boots and Donald was proud to bring home a little extra food to supplement the diet of seafood and vegetables available on the island.

It was a long walk up the track past the church and over the hill from where he looked down on the cluster of stone dwellings where the last inhabitants of Ulva struggled to survive. Thin spirals of smoke rose from the crude chimneys as the families settled in for the night. Luckily the warmer weather meant the boggy ground was now firm and the thatch was keeping the worst of the weather from entering the houses.

He and Chirsty had been so proud when they returned from their wedding ceremony in Greenock a few short years ago and moved in together. Donald had spent many hours making the dwelling livable but now it was far too small for his growing family and the shoemaker's tools.

The two eldest girls spent most of their time with Chirsty's parents, Archibald and Margaret McDonald, who had taken a dwelling close by, and the two families had survived the hard years that followed as most of the tenants were evicted from the island.

But even the back houses behind the cottages in Tobermory were more habitable than this. As he entered the crowded interior, Donald was filled with a determination to make a better life for his wife and family. In spite of her advanced pregnancy, Chirsty welcomed him with open arms. "I miss you so much when you leave the island, my Donald," she whispered.

The children sat around wide-eyed as Donald emptied his baskets. As always there was a small treat for each of them and they sat in the firelight listening to their father's story of the day's events.

Donald waited until the next morning before telling Chirsty of the ship leaving for New Zealand. "It is far too long a journey for us to undertake," he said. "I could never travel to the other side of the world and leave my parents," Chirsty agreed. "We belong here in Scotland and this is where I want to stay."

As Donald settled to work in the corner of the cottage, Chirsty gathered up the children and walked across the stubbly ground to her parents' dwelling. Ketty, John and Margaret ran ahead and she carried young Archibald straddled over her hip. "I won't be carrying you much longer my lad," she said as she swung him across her pregnant body.

Her mother rose from the seat by the fire to greet her. At 60 years of age, Margaret McDonald was still an active woman and spent much of her time spinning the fleece she gathered from the bracken fern or working with her crude knitting needles. She held up a shapeless garment as Chirsty flopped into the old rocker in the corner of the room.

"This will be a shirt for whoever it fits," she laughed. She put down her knitting and picked up her youngest grandchild. Archibald nestled close to his grandmother as she rocked him in her arms.

"Donald is talking about a ship that is to sail from Tobermory all the way to New Zealand," Chirsty said. "I fear he will want to be off one day across the sea to an unknown land. So many of our kin have left these shores already and the young men get restless when they hear of the good land and money on offer in the colonies."

"Never fear, lass. Your Donald thinks too much of his family to expect you to move so far away. No. He will remain in these parts for many a day."

Margaret was secretly pleased that her husband Archibald had never shown an interest in moving to the colonies. In fact, it was because of his stubbornness that the family still remained on Ulva, in spite of the owner, Francis Clark, endeavouring to move them. But their children were showing signs of restlessness and she knew the day would come when one or other of them would sail off to a distant land.

They heard a crunching sound outside the cottage and when the door opened it was Archibald himself, his face red from the effort of dragging a heavy bag of mussels from the shore. Margaret could tell that his joints were troubling him, although he was loathe to complain. The many hours spent gathering seaweed for the kelp harvest had taken its toll and he silently suffered from the resulting aches and pains.

Margaret threw the mussels into a large pot on the stove and let them heat for a short time until the shells opened. Then she and Chirsty skillfully extracted the flesh from the shells and placed it in a bowl ready to be turned into soup. Along with the bread made from the new flour that Donald had brought back from Tobermory and a slice of cheese, this would make an appetising lunch.

Back in her own cottage, Chirsty began to straighten the bedding on the wooden pallets and took the few dishes outside to wash them in a pail of water by the door. She thought longingly of the early days of their marriage when she had time to help her father gather the seafood which was the mainstay of their diet. Good money had once been made from the lobsters which they pulled from the creels anchored out in the bay.

But now when her father needed her more than ever, she was no longer able to assist him. Her brothers and sisters had already moved away, finding work as soon as they were old enough. "I'm not sure how much longer my father will be able to carry on fishing," she said to Donald. "But how will we survive without the food from the sea?"

"I'm thinking it's time we moved over to Mull. There would be a good living to be made in the town from mending shoes and boots as well as selling new footwear." Donald was glad of the chance to raise the subject. He had thought of little else since his return from Tobermory. "I will start looking for a suitable dwelling for us, and maybe somewhere for your parents as well."

Chirsty felt a surge of excitement. Life in Tobermory would be much more exciting than their forlorn existence on Ulva. If only her parents could be persuaded to move from the island, she would be happy to leave. There would be schooling for their children and much more opportunity for Donald to make a good living at his trade.

She was also secretly worried about the upcoming birth of her baby, due in about two months time. The pregnancy had been more difficult than the others and there would only be her mother in attendance as the woman who had acted as midwife had long gone from the island. She clasped her hands around her swollen belly but could feel little movement, unlike the other times when the unborn child had kicked and surged about.

She didn't share her worries with her husband, however. These were matters for women to keep to themselves. The two eldest children were with her mother who was teaching them their letters and basic counting. Education was important to the family as Margaret's father John Curry had been a well-respected schoolmaster on the island for many years. Margaret and Archibald had raised their children to speak in English as well as the Gaelic tongue used by most of the islanders.

"Ketty and Margaret need to be at school. Since the classroom closed at Soriby, the children who remain here are missing out on schooling," she pointed out. "Yes, I agree with you that it is time we moved to a larger village. Next time you are over on Mull you need to make enquiries. It sounds as though Tobermory or even the town of Salen would be best."

Donald smiled. He knew his wife would support him in his decision. But there were so many people moving to the villages and so few empty dwellings. It could be a long wait. He concentrated on stitching a sturdy boot, admonishing his son when he came too close.

His ambition was to have a small building in which to carry out his trade. Maybe he could expand one day and have his own cobbler's store. Now that would be something to think about. Perhaps even better than sailing off on a grand ship to the colonies.

## Chapter 2

Almost 10 years had passed since Catherine McDonald married Neil Maclougas on a bleak winter's day in the little church on Ulva. Their eldest daughter Sarah was born around eight months later, followed over the next five years by Catherine, John and Margaret. Then mercifully, the pregnancies had ceased.

"Four children is a large enough family in these uncertain times," her mother Margaret McDonald had said, until six months ago when Catherine realized she was with child once again. Although their life as crofters on Mull was a hard one, Catherine was looking forward to the new arrival. The older children were now attending school during the day and she would have time to spend with the infant.

She sat by the fireside as she waited for her husband to return with the children. Neil had volunteered to meet the young ones today as he was not needed up on the high country where the sheep grazed amongst the rocks and heather.

In fact, Neil had left home early that morning to carry out some business in Tobermory, taking a small craft from a rough wooden jetty on the north coast of the island of Mull. He was to buy some supplies from the store in the village and no doubt catch up with the news at the same time.

Catherine rose to tend to the fire and recalled her younger days on the island of Ulva when she worked as a servant for the Clark family at the mansion house. Carrying in the firewood and peat to keep the large house warm had been one of the many chores that filled her day.

She had met her husband when he visited the mansion to deliver stock to Francis Clark. As she shyly served refreshments to the good-looking stranger her heart beat faster. She felt a strong attraction, even though he was almost ten years her senior, and looked forward to his visits over the next few weeks.

After a short courtship, she and Neil had married in the small church on Ulva and settled on the larger island of Mull on a sheep and cattle property where Neil worked as a shepherd. Fortunately there was a school close by where the children learned their letters and numbers and spoke in English as well as Gaelic.

But now there was little time for day-dreaming. She could hear voices and knew that Neil and the children had returned. They crowded through the narrow doorway, all speaking at once. She hugged the youngest and took a sheet of paper from Sarah, who at the age of ten was a sensible child.

"The children are to get a new teacher," she exclaimed in surprise. "Archie Campbell is moving to Tobermory to the new school there."

She felt disappointed that they were to lose the services of Mr Campbell. He had been a strict but fair teacher and the children, who had spoken in English since the moment they could talk, were doing well in the classroom.

"Let us hope the new schoolmaster will be as well-liked as old Archie." Neil took the paper from Catherine's hand. "I see they have appointed a younger man from Oban. We will have to make him welcome and see him settled into the school teacher's house."

A small stone dwelling alongside the schoolroom served as the schoolmaster's home. The community had helped out supplying basic bedding, a table and seating. Nobody would want a teacher to feel unwelcome and he was often poorly paid.

Neil would visit the school on the morrow before heading up to the steep country to check the sheep which were due to lamb at any time. Once there he often stayed overnight in a small hut on the hillside. A ewe could easily succumb to the harsh conditions if not carefully watched at lambing time.

Catherine's own brother Alexander had helped out for a season before returning to Ulva where he worked for Francis Clark. Neil interrupted her thoughts with more urgent information. "Catherine my love, I have the most interesting news. A ship is departing from Tobermory in a

15

few short months bound for New Zealand, the land of opportunity, they say." Catherine looked at her husband in amazement. He had never shown interest in far-off places before. What had happened to change his mind?

Neil looked at his wife, due to produce a child at any time. "Never fear my dear. I would never burden you with such a journey and I hear there is unrest among the native people there. No. Our future is on Mull and this is where we will stay. At least for the moment."

Catherine felt a surge of joy. She loved her husband and would follow him to the ends of the earth, but not at this time, when the new child stirred inside her. And now it was time to plan for the meal ahead. Neil had bought some dried herrings and a loaf of crusty bread from the store, along with potatoes and corn. "We will eat well tonight," she smiled. "It will be a change from lobster and my home-made loaves."

Neil loaded wood next to the fireplace in the corner of the cottage. He knew he was in for a busy few weeks, and at times the thought of owning land and raising his own stock was a tempting one. But New Zealand? That was surely at the very end of the world.

Next morning Neil rose early and packed some food and warm clothing into a sack ready to journey up into the high ground to bring the ewes down to the shelter of the valley ready for lambing. He knew that several of the wily ones would remain behind and he would need to return to check them from time to time.

Before he left he called at the school to offer his help to move Archie Campbell's belongings down to the jetty when the time came. Archie welcomed him warmly. He had nothing but admiration for the Maclougas family.

But the schoolmaster was ready for the move to Tobermory where a comfortable cottage awaited him a short distance from the new school. "Good day to you Neil," he said as he held his hand out in greeting. "I'll be sorry to say farewell to your children, but I think the new teacher will be satisfactory. He will bring in fresh ideas and I know the people will make him welcome."

"You can be sure we will do our best," Neil promised. "But you will be sorely missed." The pair chatted for a time and Neil shared the news about the ship bound for New Zealand. "It is a great opportunity for the men folk, but a long journey for the women and children. I might consider it myself if I was a younger man with no family."

Neil's thoughts were far away as he made his way through the valley where the tufts of grass competed with heather and stunted trees. As he reached the higher land the trees made way for bracken fern and lichen and the sheep sheltered among the barren rocks.

17

As he came closer the anxious ewes clustered together and began to drift down the hillside. Others joined the mob and all Neil had to do was keep them moving, for once they were on lower ground they would be gathered together in a crude pen with walls made from rock. A makeshift gate of fern bound together would stop them from escaping while they were crutched and then released onto the lower pastures.

How good it would be to have land of his own and answer to no-one but himself. He envied the young ones who would be leaving on the great ship to New Zealand. Maybe after the bairn arrived, he and Catherine would look at making a new life in a far distant land.

# Chapter 3

The shadows were lengthening across the land as Alexander McDonald returned from the bleak shores of Ardglass to the relative comfort of Ulva Mansion House, where he shared quarters with the other farm servants.

His thoughts were with his parents and he was concerned at the state of his father's health which always worsened during the winter months. Hopefully with the warmer spring weather, his aches and pains would lessen and retrieving the lobsters from the heavy creels would become easier.

At times he wished fervently that his family would pack up and leave the dreary shores of Soriby Bay. He knew that his sister Chirsty and Donald McArthur the shoemaker were keen to move to one of the villages on Mull, but Archibald McDonald was set in his ways and vowed they would have to carry him off his beloved island in a box.

Alexander smiled at the thought. His parents had worked hard to raise a family of eight on the island. There had been many good years when a crofter's life was sustainable, and the booming kelp industry had kept many islanders employed during the season when the seaweed was burned and ground into powder to produce glass and soap.

At times Alexander felt trapped in the middle of a dilemma. On the one hand, families had been forced to leave Ulva to make way for Francis Clark's sheep and on the other he had been enticed back to work as a shepherd for the island's owner. He knew that sheep farming was the only way for Ulva to prosper but felt badly for the families forced to leave over recent years.

The proprietor's sister Johanna was outside in the yard as Alexander approached. She nodded in his direction. "My brother wishes to meet with you before the day is out," she said. Alexander was mystified. He hoped that Francis Clark was not going to ask him to persuade his parents to leave the island. Mr Clark had turned a blind eye to their presence at Ardglass during the winter months, thinking that the cold conditions and lack of food would drive them away, but along with a dozen other families, they had remained.

He stood as Alexander entered the room, beckoning him to sit on one of the wooden chairs near the fire. "Alexander McDonald," he began. "As you may have heard there is a ship leaving for New Zealand in a few months. You have been a loyal worker so if you are interested I would be willing to pay an amount towards your passage."

Alexander sat and stared at his employer, then looked out towards the distant shore. "Thank you, sir. That is indeed a kind gesture. I will go away and discuss it with my brother who is very interested in emigrating to one of the colonies. However, our preference is Canada where we have several family members already established on farmland in Ontario."

As Alexander left the room he felt a surge of excitement. He was approaching his 30th birthday and so far, no woman had succeeded in winning his heart. There was no reason why he couldn't take the opportunity to live in a new country where land was being offered to attract settlers. His brother Hugh, just a year younger than himself, would want to join him for sure.

In fact, Hugh McDonald had already read the message in the window of the store in Tobermory and was hell bent on travelling to Ulva to talk over the possibility with his brother. He arrived on the early morning boat from Mull and caught up with Alexander who was just returning from his early morning chores.

"Alex. Great news. There is the chance to go to New Zealand on a new ship sailing out of Tobermory."

"I've heard the news already. It is an exciting prospect indeed and Francis Clark has offered to assist with my passage. I think we should seriously consider it." Alexander was caught up in the excitement. "There is plenty of work on offer and the chance to own a few acres of land."

"I have other news too." Hugh's face reddened. "Mary has agreed to be my wife but I haven't yet told her of my interest in sailing to New Zealand." Alexander was pleased for his brother. Mary McKinnon was a bright and lively lass and would make a fine wife for Hugh.

"That is great news. Our mother will be thrilled. I imagine she thinks we were both destined to be single. It is easier for married men to attract sponsorship to the colonies, so you should have no trouble getting a passage."

For the first time in a while, Alexander felt a twinge of regret at not having found a wife of his own. It would be a fine thing if he and Hugh could both be married before the great ship sailed. Single women were a rare commodity in the new lands.

******************

When Hugh returned to Salen where he was employed as a herdsman, he walked into the village where he knew he would find Mary who worked as a servant at the inn. "Good evening my dear." A broad smile lit up his face as he watched Mary at work, cleaning the tables in the large dining room. "Can you get away for a short time? I have something to share with you."

Mary's face lit up as she saw Hugh enter the room. They had been courting for several months and now they were to be wed. "Of course, I have just finished for the day." She hung up her apron and went to her room to fetch a coat, as the wind was brisk outside.

Soon they were walking hand in hand through the village with its neat dwellings all built to a plan devised by Lachlan Macquarie. The stone cottages were laid out along both sides of the road through the centre of Salen, which was situated on the narrowest part of the island, where the road branched off to Gruline.

A sheltered deep water harbour gave shelter for shipping using the Sound of Mull between the island and the mainland. Standing like a sentinel on a sea cliff near the village, the ruins of Aros Castle, the ancient home of the Macdonalds, Lords of the Isles, could be seen.

As Hugh and Mary walked the length of the road, they came to the church where their marriage service would take place. Mary stood in awe of the great church with its solid stone walls. They had already spoken with the minister, the Rev Mungo Campbell. Mr Campbell was a young man, hardly older than Hugh, a keen agriculturist but not known for his eloquence. He lived in the church manse, with an elderly housekeeper and two servants and tended to talk of farming matters rather than religion.

The two families would fill the church which had been renovated a number of years before. Several family events had already been held there including the burial service for Hugh's grandfather John Curry.

"There have been baptisms and funeral services held here for my family, but I think this will be the first wedding," he said, as he drew Mary close. "My mother will be most delighted when I tell her the good news."

They wandered down to the jetty where the fishing craft were anchored and the sun was setting over the distant islands. Now Hugh took Mary's hands in his. "Mary. I have something to tell you. My brother Alex and I are keen to go on the great ship to New Zealand where there would be a grand future for us."

Mary pulled back in consternation. "But New Zealand is as far away as you can go. There would be no chance of ever coming back to Mull." Her eyes brimmed with tears. Hugh reached out for her but she turned away.

"It's all right Mary. It was only a thought. There is such a good future on offer in the colonies. I have cousins in Canada who are doing very well for themselves. It would be a fine thing if we could do the same."

But Mary was not easily persuaded. "Let's talk of other things, Hugh. Living on Mull has not prepared me for a life of uncertainty. I just want to marry and raise a family right here in Salen. Surely that is not too much to ask?"

Hugh let the subject drop. There was no point in upsetting his future wife when a voyage to New Zealand was such a slim possibility. There were marriage plans to be made and then the future could take care of itself.

# Chapter 4

Once Donald McArthur had made up his mind to move his family to Tobermory, he made enquiries with a number of people who could help him find a place to live and carry out his shoemaker's trade.

The post office at Tobermory was a great place to start and after chatting with Maggie Black, the woman who looked after the day to day running of the office, he felt more confident of finding a home for the family. The only problem was that while Archibald and Margaret McDonald remained on Ulva, Chirsty would be reluctant to leave the island.

"People are on the move all the time. I will let you know as soon as I hear of someone leaving the village," Mrs Black assured him.

Donald was also concerned about Chirsty's pregnancy. Although he said little to his wife, he noticed she was quieter than usual and often looked tired and strained, quite unlike her previous pregnancies when she had bloomed with good health. He broached the subject with her mother and Margaret, too, expressed her concern. "I think Chirsty should visit the doctor on Mull as soon as possible. Next time you go over to Mull you must take her along," she said.

But Chirsty was reluctant to make the journey. "I'll be fine as soon as the sun shines again," she said. "The long winter has drained me of all my energy." Her mother did her best to persuade Chirsty to make the journey to Tobermory, but she would not change her mind. "We have four bonny children and this one will be just as healthy."

But Chirsty was far from confident about the birth. She was loathe to admit that something might be wrong, and stubbornly insisted on carrying on as usual. She calculated that the child would be born in about two months and tried to convince herself that all would be well.

But just a day after Donald left for Mull to take his next shipment of shoes, Chirsty knew something was wrong. She woke to blood on the sheet and back pain so severe she was loathe to move from the bed. She called to the children and told them to go and fetch their grandmother who arrived soon after, banishing the young ones out the door to where Archibald was waiting.

It was soon obvious that Chirsty was in labour, but much too early and when two hours later, a tiny child was born, Margaret knew there was little hope for its survival. In fact, hardly a breath was drawn before the little girl died in Margaret's arms, a little girl they named Mary.

It was a sad scene when Donald arrived back later in the day to find an exhausted Chirsty, a dead child and Margaret grieving for a lost grandchild. Sitting in the crowded cottage that night he realised more than ever that life on Ulva looked very bleak. With four young children and the tools of his trade there was barely room to move in the dark interior. He and Archibald had buried the child in a small graveyard on the island, but no prayers were said for her as the minister could not be contacted.

Over the next few weeks, little Mary was seldom mentioned and Chirsty resumed her household tasks as though nothing had happened. She buried the grief for her dead baby somewhere deep inside and put her energies into caring for her four healthy offspring.

It was Archibald who brought the good news from Tobermory. He had called at the Ulva Inn with a basket of lobsters and there was a letter waiting for Donald McArthur. As Donald opened the letter, Archibald stayed close by, eager to learn its contents.

"Good news, father in law. Maggie Black at the post office has spoken with the owners of two cottages in Argyll Terrace. The occupants are moving out soon to settle on the mainland and our name has been put forward as possible tenants."

Archibald reeled at the announcement. As long as he could remember, he had resisted all efforts to remove him from Ulva, where he had lived for most of his 75 years. The sights and sounds of the island were his life blood. Yet he knew the move to Mull would be the making of Donald McArthur and his family. The children needed schooling that was no longer available with the closure of the classroom and there would be much more call for a shoemaker in the village.

Putting on a brave face, Archibald shook Donald by the hand. "Tobermory would be good for your trade and your children. I will discuss the idea with Margaret and see what she has to say." And he left Donald standing in the room, the letter still clutched in his hand.

Chirsty's pale face lit up at the news. "If a place could be found for my parents, I would be most happy to move to Tobermory," she said. "I'm sure we could afford the extra rent with the increase in your shoe repairs, and my father may find a job on the lobster boats."

After the loss of her baby, Chirsty knew a change of lifestyle would be a good thing and she was keen to make the move as long as her father could be persuaded to leave the island of Ulva.

Before their marriage, she and Donald had worked hard to make their simple home livable, but now the grim stone walls and fragile thatch felt like a prison. The fire in the centre of the room provided a little light, but the interior was smoky. How good it would be to live in a cottage with windows and a real chimney to allow the smoke to escape.

She straightened the bedding on the straw pallets and folded the garments of clothing that were strewn on the beds. The two older girls, Ketty and Margaret, usually slept at her parents' house leaving John and young Archibald to share the dwelling with Donald and Chirsty. Even so, the interior was cluttered and disorganized.

"Imagine having a place for your shoemaker's tools and leather. People will call and order new shoes and boots and everyone will want to see your new footwear designs," Chirsty enthused. "I just know life will be so much better if we move to Tobermory."

Donald sighed with relief. It seemed that his dream of moving off the island was to come true. The thought of the ship sailing to New Zealand still tempted him but in the meantime, he could build up his business in Tobermory and provide a better life for his wife and family.

When Archibald McDonald left Donald and Chirsty's dwelling, he walked sadly down to the water's edge to gaze out over the calm waters of Soriby Bay. The sun was low in the sky and he stood deep in thought, remembering all the good years on the island of Ulva. First he had lived high on the hills at Ferinardry, when a crofter could make a living from the land. Later the family had moved to Soriby where most of his income came from the sea.

The latest move to Ardglass had been a desperate attempt to stay on the island, long after Francis Clark had warned all the families to move. Starvation Terrace it was called and for many families it proved to be the last straw, with the failure of crops and the demise of the kelp industry.

Archibald's eyes misted over as he remembered the joy of raising a healthy family and seeing them grow to adulthood. So far, none had travelled further afield than Oban on the mainland, but Archibald was sure the call of the colonies would eventually be too strong, and one or more of his children would sail to a distant land.

# Chapter 5

With the thought of travelling to New Zealand on his mind, the days went by slowly for Alexander McDonald who grew impatient to learn more about the prospects in the new land. Francis Clark had given him some papers to read with details of life in the colonies.

He shared this information with his brother who said little. Since his confrontation with Mary, Hugh had not mentioned New Zealand to her again, but he grew more frustrated as he read the documents. "Twenty acres of land, promise of employment, assistance with building a place to live." It sounded too good to be true.

"Hugh, New Zealand is the place for us." Alexander was enthusiastic. "You are more fortunate than I as you will have a wife to share the new venture. Maybe I should look around and find a likely partner before the date of sailing." Alexander laughed. He knew there were a number of wenches who would be more than pleased to accompany him to New Zealand.

Each time he returned to Francis Clark's farm where he lived with the other servants, he felt the eyes of Sally Lamont, the outdoor servant, upon him. Sally was a bonny lass, and would make a good wife he was sure, but so far they had been little more than friends, apart from a quick kiss on special occasions.

With the thought of a grand future on the other side of the world, Alexander looked at Sally with different eyes. Finding her milking the last of the cows, he offered to help carry the heavy pail of milk into the dairy behind the house.

"Alex, has the sun got to your head? You've never offered to carry the milk before." Sally blushed and handed him the heavy pail. "Surely there must be a favour you're after." She stood, hands on hips, watching as Alexander walked away, whistling loudly to cover his embarrassment.

As she led the cow back to the enclosed pasture, Sally was puzzled. She'd set her sights on the handsome herdsman many months before. Perhaps he was starting to notice her attentions. She removed the heavy apron she wore and smoothed her clothing.

At 27 years she was beginning to think that marriage had passed her by, but with Alexander, who was several years her senior, there could well be a match. She followed him into the dairy and leaned against the long bench that ran along one wall.

"All right, Alex my love, what is it you want from me?" She looked up and saw that Alexander was in no hurry to leave. He smiled as he took in her arrogant stance. Oh yes, she could well be the woman to claim as his bride.

Sally was a strong woman who would be a match for anyone who got in her way. Alexander stepped towards her and took her in his arms. Their kiss was long and passionate and filled with the promise of more to come.

*********************

When Hugh McDonald was next with Mary he was loathe to mention the ship bound for New Zealand. They spoke of wedding dates and guests and where they were to live after their marriage, but Hugh's heart was not really in it. He could see no future on Mull for the next generation. In New Zealand they could be free to own land and have wealth beyond his wildest dreams.

"Are you not listening to me Hugh?" Mary asked as she listed the folk to be invited to the wedding celebrations. "Do you want your Maclougas family to come to the wedding or just the McDonalds, and of course, the McKinnons on my side?"

Hugh answered with no emotion. "You plan it the way you want my dear," and he left it at that. He gazed out across the water to the far distant islands. Was he always to be a shepherd, herding someone else's animals, or could he one day have stock of his own?

*****************

Francis Clark was all in favour of his employee Alexander McDonald taking advantage of the chance of a new life in New Zealand. He had been patient in the extreme as Alexander's parents, old Archibald and Margaret, had remained on Ulva, defying the odds. He had also respected the older sister Catherine who had served in the household a few years previously, before marrying Neil Maclougas.

Yes, Francis Clark wanted the best for this family. Of all the people he had inherited, these were gentle folk, thanks to the education gleaned from Margaret's father, the schoolmaster, John Curry.

He noticed that young Alexander was spending more time with the servant lass, Sally Lamont. "It is time that young man found himself a wife," he said to his sister, as he knew that married men were better accepted in the colonies. He smiled as he noticed the clumsy way that Alexander was trying to find favour with the young woman. Carrying the milk bucket indeed! Now that was a sight to warm the heart.

The sun struggled through the clouds next day as Alexander made his way along the narrow path towards the top pastures. From here he could see the ruins of Soriby where he had spent much of his childhood. Little remained of the settlement apart from the rock walls of the dwellings which protruded from the stubbly grass and fern.

Further up the hill he paused to look down on the bleak shores of Soriby Bay and the few remaining cottages at Ardglass. It would be strange to leave these familiar sights for ever. He would like to have called on his parents and sister, but he had stock to check and no time to loiter. The ewes would lamb soon and before then he needed to keep a close eye on the flock.

He checked the familiar hillsides and rocky outcrops where the sheep tended to shelter from the wind and rain. A few startled animals ran off as he approached but most remained calmly grazing and barely lifted their heads as he moved down the steep slopes back towards the trail which led to the lonely church.

His younger brothers and sisters had all been baptized here. Before the church was built the minister had been invited to perform the ceremony at the new child's home, usually joining in the feasting and partying that was part of the christening ritual.

Alexander paused outside the gate, then entered the small wooden and stone building which was rarely used these days. The door creaked as he pushed it open and he breathed in the musty air. Maybe he could get married here and bring the small church back to life, as he and his bride celebrated their wedding day with friends and family once more filling the wooden seats.

He felt a surge of excitement as he remembered Sally's warm kiss and soft body. "Sally, my love, I want to make you mine." He spoke the words aloud and they reverberated around the wooden walls. Filled with purpose, he strode from the church and along the trail back to the cluster of buildings which made up Ulva Mansion House.

# Chapter 6

The first rays of sun were piercing the clouds as Mary Ann Maclougas was born with a rush that took the midwife by surprise. Margaret McDonald was alongside and caught the red, squirming bundle as Catherine gave a final desperate heave.

After five years she had almost forgotten the pain of birth and lay exhausted and sweating from her labour. Margaret, however, was delighted at the sight of the healthy, noisy child after the previous sad birth a few days before.

"We'll name her Mary after Chirsty's tiny child," Catherine said, as soon as her mother held up the baby for her to inspect. "And of course, to honour your mother, Mary Curry and your sister Ann." Catherine extended her arms to take her new daughter and lay back in relief that her ordeal was over.

Margaret was happy to hear that there was to be another child to carry on her mother's name and that of her sister Ann who had died in Salen more than ten years previously. Ann's husband John, a joiner who had rebuilt the church in the village, had later erected a fine memorial stone at

Pennygown graveyard for his wife and her father, the schoolmaster John Curry.

As the midwife took her leave, Neil Maclougas put his head around the doorway. "I'm told we have a healthy new daughter, dear Catherine," he said as he stood awkwardly just inside the room.

He came closer to see the new child and Margaret stood aside to give the new parents time to admire the little girl. Tears filled her eyes as she thought of Chirsty's dead baby. She knew that soon Chirsty would have to be told of her sister's new daughter, also named Mary.

In the meantime there were four hungry children to be fed before they left for school. Young Sarah was already awake and staring in amazement at her new sister. The others soon joined her and stood in a circle around the wooden cradle in which their father had placed the infant.

"She's so small and she's got a very red face," Sarah observed. John glared at his new sister in disgust. Surely he could have had a little brother. "Can't we take her back and get a boy?" he said, and his father laughed and took his hand for a moment. "It's just you and me son, to look after all these women."

After they had eaten a meal of broth and warm bread, Neil set off to the schoolhouse with his children. The new school teacher had already arrived and was being assisted on his first day by Archie Campbell. Angus McLean was tall and lean but looked anxious as he faced his pupils for the first time.

He need not have worried however, as the children well well-mannered and attentive and he relaxed visibly as the morning went on. He could see that their old teacher was a good disciplinarian and had taught his pupils well.

As they stopped for a meal at mid-day, Angus was confident that he was well equipped for the task that lay ahead, especially when Archie Campbell produced an accordion and the children responded in a tuneful fashion, with an old Gaelic air.  Much to the delight of their new teacher, the children sang and tapped their toes to the beat.
Then their new teacher came out with a fiddle of his own and joined in with a harmony that had all heads turning in his direction. The pupils were spell-bound. The music they loved would continue with Angus McLean at the helm.


*******************


When Margaret returned to Ulva a few days later, she was careful not to display too much pleasure at the birth of a new grand-daughter. Although Chirsty was hiding her feelings well, her mother knew that the grieving for the dead child was far from complete.

When Chirsty was told of the birth of her sister's child, she was pleased that the bairn was alive and well. "So she is to be named Mary Ann. At least our grandmother's name will live on," she said when her mother told her the news.

"I am truly happy for Catherine and Neil. You must believe me," Chirsty insisted, but her mother could sense an underlying tension. "It just seems such a waste that my daughter lived for such a short time. But now there is another Mary to take her place." And as Chirsty said the words, the tears flowed and as she sobbed in Margaret's arms, she felt a sense of relief. She had been holding back her sadness for much too long but now it was time to move on.

*********************

As the spring days turned into summer, Neil was busy out on the high country tending the sheep that had been left behind. Once in a while he helped a ewe in trouble but mostly it was a case of making sure none were tangled in the thick undergrowth.

In the meantime, little Mary Ann thrived in her mother's care and the older children enjoyed lessons with their latest teacher. Angus McLean was relishing in his new environment. Back on the mainland in Oban he had taught the children

41

of fishermen and labourers. Now he was dealing with country children with an innocence that was appealing.

In particular young Sarah Maclougas showed a musical talent beyond her years. As well as playing the fiddle with dexterity she sang with the voice of an angel and her teacher was certain she was destined for a great future.

Whenever Neil Maclougas visited the school to collect the children,  Angus was full of praise for Sarah's musical ability. "Believe me, I have never seen such talent in a young child."

"We are so fortunate to have fine, healthy children." Neil often said the words as Catherine sat in the rocker, nursing little Mary Ann, with the older girls gathered around. John was still inclined to sulk that the newest arrival had not been a boy, but Neil made much of his son's ability to carry out the chores while he was out on the hills.

"We would not manage without you, son," he often said. "You have to look after the family when I am away tending the flock.

## Chapter 7

For Chirsty McArthur, the news of the birth of a daughter to Catherine and Neil Maclougas brought back painful memories of her own sad loss. On the one hand she was relieved that the new child had arrived safely, yet on the other it filled her with melancholy as she remembered her own daughter who had survived for such a brief time.

"I know that I will be reminded of our dead child every time I see little Mary Ann," Chirsty confided to her mother. It was hard to settle to the work that was piling up around her. There was firewood and peat to gather for the stove and candles and soap to make from the oily fat.

The winter months had left the ground around the cottage bare and every shower of rain turned the earth into mud. Chirsty and the older children spent many hours gathering shell from the shoreline to form a path. This would keep the worst of the mud and grime from being trampled onto the boards that covered most of the dirt floor.

But the sun grew warmer each day and the bluebells bloomed in the fields colouring the drab landscape, Ketty and Margaret loved to gather the wild roses that grew in abundance and Chirsty's desolate mood began to lift.

But she still worried at the lack of schooling for her children and waited impatiently for news to come through about a cottage in Tobermory. Her husband Donald was feeling even more frustrated. As he listened to Christy's brothers' plans to take the ship to New Zealand his restlessness grew.

If his family was not destined to make the long journey to the other side of the world, at least he could make a good living for them in the busy village on Mull. Each time he called at the post shop in Tobermory he was anxious for news of the availability of the cottages in Argyll Terrace.

He had almost given up hope when Maggie Black rushed out to greet him one morning and gave him the good news. "You have been accepted as tenants for the Argyll Terrace cottages. There is an empty dwelling for you and another next door with a spare room for a couple."

Almost in a daze, Donald walked up the steep track to the Upper Village, hardly able to believe his luck. He stood at the gate of the sturdy stone cottage overlooking the bay, so close to the church and school. There was a small building in the back yard, just right for his shoemaking tools.

If he couldn't take his family to the colonies this would be his second choice. He knew Chirsty and the children would thrive in this environment and Archibald and Margaret would hopefully settle next door. Yes, this was certainly a golden day.

When he returned to the primitive dwelling at Ardglass that night his excitement mounted. "Chirsty my love, we're on the move. No more drudgery in a smoke-filled hovel for you. We're moving to Tobermory as soon as you are ready."

Chirsty could hardly take in what he was saying. Now she had to help her parents come to terms with the decision to move. Her mother would be happy to leave the island but she was not so sure about her father. Archibald was inclined to be set in his ways and leaving his beloved island of Ulva would be a huge wrench.

***********************

When the time came to leave for Tobermory, there were many hands to make light work of the move. Alexander and Hugh were able to take a day off work to help their parents and sister load their possessions onto a small boat and row them around to the Ulva jetty where the ferry would pick them up later in the day.

It didn't take long for Archibald and Margaret to pack their few household goods and the precious spinning wheel, and Chirsty's family had gathered a mound of clothing and bedding over the years. The shoemaking tools were carefully loaded with Donald McArthur anxiously supervising.

"I'd hate to see these precious tools end up at the bottom of the bay," he said. "I plan to be setting up business in the small back house behind the cottage."

Chirsty and the children piled bundles of bedding on top of the tools and pots and pans. Their only furniture, a wooden table and two long seats, were left behind. "We'll find something better than this in Tobermory," promised Donald, as Chirsty looked on.

The children were full of excitement, with Ketty and Margaret keeping watch over little Archibald who was clutching a piece of tattered cloth. "Come along Archie. Your grandmother will make you a special blanket when we get to the new house," Chirsty promised, as she lifted him onto her hip for the walk around to the jetty.

As the ferry pulled away from the shore and headed towards Mull, Archibald sat in the stern and looked back towards Ulva. Clouds were gathering sulkily over the hills and he could just make out the bleak dwellings at Ardglass where a handful of families still struggled to survive. He had vowed that this day would never come, but he had begun to realise it was time to put the needs of his family ahead of his own.

He looked at his children who had come to help today and the bright-eyed grandchildren who would have much more opportunity in Tobermory. "I believe we are doing the right thing Margaret," he admitted. His wife breathed a sigh of relief. So far, Archibald seemed to be accepting the move. "I know we have no choice but to leave Ulva," she replied, taking him by the hand. "I'm sure we will live out our days happily on Mull."

The sun was setting over the distant islands, when Archibald and Margaret were finally settled in the cottage in Argyll Terrace. They were to have the upper level of the house, sharing the kitchen area with the present tenant, John McInnes, a fine old gentleman of eighty years who slept in a small room downstairs.

But tonight they would share a meal with Donald and Chirsty in the house next door. The boys had carried the shoemaking gear out to the small back house and Alexander had found a plank of wood to use as a table and boxes for seats which they arranged in the living area.

"This is a palace fit for a queen," Chirsty rejoiced. She could visualize curtains at the windows and a rocking chair beside the fireplace. "Thank you dear Donald for making this possible."

Before darkness fell, they gathered fern which grew in abundance on the hill behind the graveyard and piled it into makeshift beds. Their worn old blankets were thrown over the fern and Chirsty and Donald fell into an exhausted sleep.

The children woke early next morning, to the unaccustomed sound of a rooster crowing. Voices could be heard outside and the rumble of wooden wheels on the cobbled street. Donald walked down the hill to the village to buy a loaf and some dried fish and a large hunk of cheese. By the time he returned, Chirsty had the fire lit for the cooking stove and the children were dressed and eager to explore their new neighbourhood.

There would be no shortage of playmates as the narrow lane behind the dwellings was filled with children, today being Saturday and a day away from the classroom. The girls stood shyly inside the fence, but John was soon out running with the other boys chasing a ball made from cow hide.

Margaret McDonald was hanging laundry on a makeshift line and looked over the fence at the gaggle of children. "I see young John is happy already," she smiled. "I'm sure the girls will find friends too when they start school next week."

Chirsty agreed. "They are not used to so many people. They are likely to feel shy and awkward in company." She joined Donald who had set up his last and tools in the back house at the rear of the cottage. A narrow lane ran behind the building and would be ideal for customers calling to have their shoes and boots repaired.

He smiled when she entered and took her in his arms. "This is already so much better than life on Ulva. We should have made the move years ago. I will be able to start making shoes to measure as well as filling the orders for the leather store."

# Chapter 8

Almost a month went by before Catherine and Neil Maclougas were able to take the children to visit their grandparents in Tobermory. Neil had been busy with lambing and they wanted baby Mary Ann to be a little older before taking the boat around the coast to the town.

Chirsty and Donald were at the jetty to meet the family and helped them off the small craft. The cousins were wildly excited to meet again as it had been many months since the MacLougas family had visited Ulva. Chirsty's eyes filled with tears as she held out her arms to take the small child. Mary Ann gave her an uncertain smile and Chirsty gently touched the small face which peeped out from under a warm woollen bonnet.

"She's so beautiful Catherine. I would like to keep her for ever," she smiled. Donald glanced at her with some concern but could see that the sight of her sister's baby did not appear to be too upsetting for his wife. "Congratulations, Neil. She really is a bonny child," he acknowledged to the proud father. "But I know her grandparents are most anxious to see her."

The older children ran ahead up the steep road and were soon bursting into the door of the McArthurs' cottage where their grandparents were impatiently waiting to greet them. "Come along in my dears," Margaret greeted them as old Archibald hovered in the background. "Come and see Chirsty and Donald's fine new home."

Chirsty showed Catherine the cooking stove and the furniture Donald and Archibald had fashioned from the wood and boxes. They climbed the steep steps up to the second floor where the children's bedding was spread out on wooden pallets. Catherine was happy for her sister as this cottage was certainly far superior to the dwellings on Ulva with their damp stone walls and smoky fires.

Neil was taken out into the back house and was soon admiring the shoemaker's workshop with its pile of leather and the half finished shoes and boots. "You will do so well here in the village, Donald. It won't be long before everyone in town will be buying your footwear."

"That may be so Neil, but money is scarce and not many villagers can afford to buy new boots. I already sell more on the mainland in Oban than in Tobermory itself. I do worry at times about our future here on Mull. It seems the colonies offer far more opportunity for our children."

Neil agreed. "I would be off tomorrow if it weren't for Catherine and the children. I fear that our children will be moving away as soon as they are old enough." But the serious talk was soon drowned out by the laughter of the children as they ran in the lane behind the cottages and down the road to see the school which the McArthur children now attended.

"Our teacher is Mr Campbell and his house is just along the street," Ketty told her cousins. Sarah was excited at the thought that her former teacher lived close by. "He was very good to us, but could be stern if you were late or untidy with your writing," she warned. When they told their father that Archie Campbell was living close by, Neil took a few moments to call and visit his old friend who was now well settled in his new home.

"There are some bright youngsters here and it is a treat to be teaching the older pupils and knowing the young ones are being taught by a young woman who can give them more attention than I ever could." Archie thought back to his days in the one crowded classroom where the children were of all ages.

He had introduced more music into the daily programme and was anxious to hear how the MacLougas children were faring with their new teacher. "Is young Sarah still singing like an angel?" Archie wanted to know and was relieved when her father said she was using her talent at every opportunity.

"Aye, she has a fine voice for one so young. It would be good if she could come to Tobermory to be taught when she is a little older. Perhaps she could stay with the McArthurs or with her grandparents?"

Neil agreed to consider the idea but knew that Catherine would miss the help with the other children if Sarah was to leave home too soon. "I will discuss it with my wife, but Sarah is a little too young to leave home yet," he said. Neil was happy that the schoolmaster had settled well into life in Tobermory. Chirsty and Donald's children would now have the opportunity to learn from his many years of experience.

"My wife's nieces and nephew have missed out on their education whilst living on Ulva, but they are bright youngsters and should soon catch up with their peers," said Neil, shaking Archie Campbell by the hand. Soon he returned to the noisy cottage where the families were gathered around the table. Old Margaret was cradling little Mary Ann in her arms and Catherine was catching up on the family news.

"Is it true you're off to New Zealand?" she asked her brothers when she had a moment alone with them. "It's a big step to take, but I know my husband would be gone if he had the chance."

Both young men shot secretive glances towards their mother who had not yet been told of their plans. "The idea is still in its infancy, and we haven't told our parents yet," Hugh admitted. "And don't breathe a word of it to my bride-to-be who will need a great deal of persuasion before she will agree to leaving these shores."

It was almost dark before the Maclougas family took their leave and boarded the small craft to take them back around the shores to the northern tip of Mull. The children were tired from the excitement of the day and little Mary Ann slept all the way, snuggled warmly in the thick wool blanket which her grandmother had knitted for her. Their small stone dwelling looked a little bleak after the cottages in Tobermory, but with a warm fire on the hearth and a pot of broth bubbling, Neil and Catherine sat with their children, discussing the day's events until the candles were spluttering and the moon rose over the bay.

"Tobermory is a place I like to visit, but it is a little crowded for me," said Neil as he lay beside his wife that night. "If we made the move it would be to an empty land with space to move and fresh air to breathe."

Catherine remained silent. She could sense a restlessness in Neil but she wasn't ready to take up the challenge of a new life in an unknown land. She worried at her parents' reaction if young Alexander and Hugh left for far-away places. But they would fare well with no children to burden them. Yes. Leave it up to the young men to settle on other shores.

# Chapter 9

The visit to Tobermory had been more unsettling to Neil MacLougas than he would have believed possible. For generations his family had been content to live off the land in the rugged coastal environment of the Scottish islands, but times were changing and young men were beginning to expect more out of life.

With a wife and five young children to provide for, Neil was feeling the burden of responsibility, and felt envious that Catherine's brothers had the chance to find a new life in the colonies.

He looked across at Catherine as she sat by the fireside, the embers casting a warm glow on her face. She was feeding little Mary Ann and the sight sent a stirring through his body. It was too soon after the birth to lie with his wife. For the time being he made do with a rough pallet of straw on one of the narrow wooden benches along the wall of the dwelling.

To cover up his feelings, he gave Catherine a quick caress on the top of her head and went outside to wash in the basin of water beside the door. The distant mountains partially blocked out the light from the moon casting strange shadows on the land. This was his birthplace, his home, yet he gained no comfort from the thought.

There was an exciting new world out there with much to offer. Perhaps the time had come to join the ever-growing number of families who were leaving for distant shores.

*********************

By the time Catherine woke next morning, Neil was already out on the hillside tending the flock. She sighed as she lifted the heavy pot of oatmeal from the hook over the fire and placed it on the sturdy wooden table.

"It's time to eat," she called to the sleepy-eyed children as they rolled from their beds. "Then it's off to school with you." Sarah and young Catherine were first to the table, Sarah ladling out the porridge for them both. After the late return from Tobermory, the younger children, Margaret and John, were loathe to leave their beds so their mother thought it best to let them sleep longer even if it meant a day off school.

After being in her sister Chirsty's house the day before, Catherine felt discontented with her lot. Since the arrival of the new infant, the cramped little dwelling seemed smaller than ever, and she felt a stab of envy when she pictured Chirsty with her fine cooking stove and the sleeping space up in the loft.

With the baby needing attention and food to prepare for the children's mid-day meal, Catherine was soon caught up in the never-ending round of chores. Today she would wash the clothing in the little stream that ran beside the cottage and hang the garments over the clean rocks to dry in the sun.

She knew that moving to Tobermory was not an option for her family, as Neil was a shepherd and needed to work on the land. With all this talk of her brothers planning to emigrate, it was creating a feeling of discontent amongst the rest of the family.

Catherine banged the clothing harder onto the rocks as she lathered the stubborn dirt with soap rendered down from mutton fat. She thought about her parents who had just moved to Mull after living all those years on the barren shores of Ulva. How would old Archibald adapt to the new lifestyle? She smiled at the thought of his stubbornness but knew her mother Margaret would thrive in the Argyll Terrace cottage.

But now Margaret and John were demanding lunch and little Mary Ann would be ready for her next feed. There was little time to ponder about other people's lives.

***********************

With a roomful of eager youngsters, the new schoolmaster, Angus McLean was revelling in his new position at the small seaside school on Mull. These were gentle children compared to the rowdy offspring of fishermen and seafarers he had taught in the larger town of Oban across the water.

With their main lessons over for the days, it was time to enjoy some music, and the children squirmed in their seats in anticipation at the lively session ahead. For Sarah MacLougas, in particular, this was the best part of the day. With the teacher playing the fiddle, she sang with a voice developed well beyond her years, the notes as sweet and pure as a song-bird.

Angus McLean knew he was listening to a rare talent in one so young. It was his ambition to teach each of his pupils to play a musical instrument and to train a small group to sing the ancient Scottish melodies. He would ask their former teacher to help them travel to Tobermory to sing at the Ceilidh held in the village each summer.

With this in mind he encouraged the children to spend time outside the classroom, listening to the voices of nature. They would lie on the mossy grass and look up at the drifting clouds and open their ears to the sound of the waves pounding the shore, the gulls screeching in the bay and the wind rustling the grass and bushes around them.

"You are hearing the wind song," he said. "It is the sweet sound of nature, and travels with you wherever you may go." Angus had dreamed of becoming a musician, but with no money for lessons or travel, he had taken up teaching. While at times it was a dreary existence, he was glad when the work offered the chance to encourage others to make use of their talents.

The children were learning a new song today, with Sarah to sing the verse and the others joining her in the chorus. Angus had composed the simple tune, and the lyrics spoke of the song of the seas, and the stars and far-away lands.

As Sarah sang the words, the children in the small room were hushed: *"The gentle breeze carries the sound of water and rustling leaves... The call of the gulls and voices, soft and full of love."*

Angus joined in, pulling his bow across the strings of the fiddle, and when the children began to sing the chorus he knew he had created something magical.

# Chapter 10

When Archie Campbell opened the letter from the young schoolmaster, Angus McLean, he felt a surge of excitement. So, his former pupils were keeping up their musical skills and wanted to travel to Tobermory to perform in the Ceilidh later in the month.

It should be easy to arrange places for the children to stay while they were in town. In fact, beds could be made up in the school rooms and meals prepared by the Tobermory women for the few days they would spend in the village.

He folded the letter and placed it on the table, then picked up his hat and walked briskly along the narrow path towards the McArthurs' cottage. Donald and Chirsty would have some ideas about the project as Chirsty's niece, Sarah Maclougas would no doubt be playing a big part in its success.

Chirsty was preparing a meal for the family when the schoolmaster arrived, but invited him in cordially. "To what do we owe the pleasure of a visit from such a busy man as yourself?" she queried.

Archie Campbell told her of the letter and soon the two of them were working out the details. "You are right. The children would be better off staying together at the school and we can all provide bedding and food for them to eat," Chirsty said.

Chirsty was happy at the prospect of her gifted niece performing at the Ceilidh. She had often thought that such a talent should be aired and not buried away in a small crofting community. "I'm sure my mother Margaret would be only to pleased to help with the arrangements," she added. "Time is lying heavily on her hands since she moved from Ulva."

In fact, Chirsty was right. Since moving to Tobermory, Margaret McDonald was finding that she had more time to spare. No longer did it take all day to complete her household chores, even though she was providing the meals for old John McInnes who slept next to the living area on the lower floor.

She also helped Chirsty with the two youngest children, while Ketty and Margaret were finally settling into their school routine. Little Archibald was a lively child, always on the move, while young John liked to help his father out in the small back house where he was busy making and repairing footwear for the villagers.

Margaret was relieved that old Archibald had been able to find work on the lobster boats that left the jetty each day. Although he was not as strong or agile as the younger men, his many years of experience were welcome as the boat left the bay to clear the lobster creels along the rocky shoreline.

When Chirsty told her mother of the proposed visit by the children from Sarah's school, Margaret said she would help with the arrangements. "It will be so good to see the children and hear them sing at the Ceilidh. I will ask the women at the church to help with the food and bedding."

Margaret and Archibald had wasted no time in joining the nearby church, which stood on the hillside at the end of their road. With Chirsty and Donald McArthur's family also swelling the ranks, the small church was filled to overflowing for the Sunday services.

Once she had heard about the children singing at the Ceilidh, Margaret spoke to the other parishioners who gathered outside the church after the service. She was surprised at the mixed reception to her ideas.

"We don't know these children. They may be ill-kempt and badly behaved," said one woman. "I would be against strangers staying in our school rooms."

Margaret was aghast at the reaction. She knew that the children at the small school were very well disciplined and would be extremely quiet and shy in the larger village of Tobermory. She felt a little dispirited until one woman voiced the opposite opinion.

"I see nothing wrong with the idea and would welcome these youngsters into the village." It was Mary McNeil who spoke, loudly enough to be heard above the others.

"I agree," said another. "The children should be encouraged to display their talents."

Soon each of the women was expressing an opinion and the men folk gathered around to see what all the fuss was about. Archibald smiled when he realised what was going on. He knew that once his wife made up her mind about something nothing would get in her way.

He turned to his son-in-law, Donald McArthur, slapping him on the shoulder. "They don't know our Margaret as we do. Those children will be staying in the school rooms, mark my words."

The two men left the women arguing and made their way across the roughly paved road to the end of Argyll Terrace where they stood gazing out over Tobermory Bay.

"It seems this new life is not such a bad one," Archibald admitted. "I'm already earning more money on the lobster boats and your children are settling into the school routine."

Donald smiled. He had felt a little guilty at persuading the old man to leave Ulva, but he was adapting to village life more readily than anyone would have thought possible.

"I'm pleased for you, Archibald. Chirsty and I were loathe to take you from your precious island, but life is certainly better for all of us since we made the move."

63

Donald had not totally given up the idea of sailing on the great ship to New Zealand, and envied the younger men when they talked of the adventure ahead. But life as a shoemaker in Tobermory was keeping him busy for the time being.

Although Chirsty had not mentioned it, he was certain that she was once again with child. The love-making they shared had become spasmodic and her breasts were tender to the touch. He sighed as he thought of the child they had lost so recently and prayed that this bairn would be born healthy and strong.

At least there was more space in the new cottage for another child. He would see to it that Chirsty was kept comfortable and not over-burdened during this pregnancy.

Margaret McDonald was also aware of her daughter Chirsty's pregnancy. She often thought sadly of the tiny infant who had arrived too early such a short time ago. She hoped for Chirsty's sake that this new child would be born safely.

All she could do was help with the heavy work around the Argyll Terrace cottages and keep the younger children from under her daughter's feet. She was pleased that old Archibald had adapted to living in the village, but knew that the coming winter months would be the test, as his joints stiffened and his movements became slower. She

knew that the hard life of a lobsterman would not
be possible for too much longer.

# Chapter 11

Since moving to the cottage in Argyll Terrace Margaret McDonald had quickly settled into her new life in the village of Tobermory.

Her weaving loom was often in use as she finished the last of the fleece painstakingly gathered while on the smaller island of Ulva, and it was time to start searching for a new supply. She would ask Alexander to bring over more supplies from Francis Clark's fine flock of sheep but he seemed reluctant to visit these days.

"That young man has something on his mind," she confided to Archibald. "Maybe he is annoyed at us leaving him behind on Ulva. It is probably time he moved on himself. As much as I would hate to see any of our children leave, there's a wide world out there with much more opportunity for the younger generation."

Archibald reluctantly agreed. He had heard remnants of the conversations between the brothers and knew they were being tempted by the chance to travel to distant shores.

"You are right, dear Margaret. These young ones want to explore a much wider world than we ever did. To think, some poor souls have never travelled further than the island of Mull. They have no concept of a world beyond these shores."

Margaret smiled, remembering the lessons she had learned from her father, John Curry. He may not have travelled far but he had mixed with men who had made long journeys and over the years had helped writers and scholars compile their great works.

She knew the time would come when one or other of their children would follow her own Curry family who were making new lives for themselves in Ontaria, Canada. Yes, her brother Charles and sister Bell and their families were well settled in the new land.

With time on her hands and the sun shining through the clouds, Margaret pulled on a shawl and bonnet and made her way up the steep hill behind the graveyard, to the outskirts of the village.

Here sheep and shaggy Highland cattle grazed and she searched the bushes for fragments of wool to boost her dwindling supplies. The bramble bushes and bracken fern were always the best source of supply as the sheep sought shelter from the wind that blew in from the bay.

Soon she had filled a cloth bag with the multi-coloured fleece and rested for a time before walking back down the hillside. From here she could see the small islands further out in the harbour and she thought for a moment of their former home on Ulva. She wondered how the remaining families were faring on the desolate shores at Ardglass, and whether they had finally been forced to abandon the dreary dwellings.

She had tried to find places on Mull for some of her former neighbours, but most were paupers with no way of paying the rent. Even the little back houses behind the cottages in Tobermory were beyond their means. What was to become of the children, as many as five or six in some of the dwellings, with no schooling and little to eat?

"I am so lucky to have my family to help us survive," she thought. She knew that without the help of Donald and Chirsty, she and Archibald would still be living a bleak existence. She also knew that she could not forget the people they had left behind. One day soon she would approach the leaders of the community and try to find a solution to the problem.

As she walked slowly back to the village she looked out for any empty or abandoned dwellings, no matter how humble. Families forced to leave the smaller islands had crowded into Tobermory, living in many of the small back houses built to shelter the animals. Donald was making use of one of these for his shoemaker's business, but there were many families living in these crowded conditions, glad to have a roof over their heads.

Women stood in their doorways, as the children played in the lanes between the houses. In spite of the conditions, there was a sense of community beginning to build up here, although the older residents were far from happy. The calm of their quiet village was being shattered by these outsiders.

Margaret could understand their initial reluctance at letting the visiting children use the school rooms during the Ceilidh which was due to begin in a month's time. As she passed the home of her new friend Mary McNeil, who had supported her efforts to accommodate the children, she paused at the gateway. Was it too soon to visit unannounced?

As she hesitated, Mary came to the doorway, her worn face breaking into a smile at the sight of Margaret. "You must come in and share a warm drink," she said. The interior was dark as the curtains were drawn and Margaret could just make out an old man sitting in a chair beside the stove.

"Meet my father, Angus McNeil." Mary introduced them. "Margaret and her family have recently moved into Argyll Terrace and are proving to be a great asset to our village." Margaret moved towards the elderly man and took his frail hand.

"We were unwilling to leave Ulva, where we lived for many years and raised our family, but the changing times finally caught up with us," she said. "However, life is treating us well in Tobermory and we are most fortunate to have found such a fine dwelling."

"Aye lass, times are certainly changing and I too was reluctant to make the move from the hill country to the town." Angus stared ahead and Margaret could see that he was probably almost blind. "But I am fortunate to have such a caring daughter who has made room for me in her household."

Over a cup of strong tea, the two women discussed the plans for hosting the children and agreed that a meeting should be held in the next few days to make final arrangements. The whole village was looking forward to the celebrations which attracted many visitors to the town. Rooms at the hotels and rooming houses were in big demand as the occasion brought together the musical talent of several of the nearby islands.

Margaret felt a sense of pride that her granddaughter Sarah would be part of the entertainment and have the chance to perform in front of such a large audience. But there was much to do to prepare for the big event. There was bedding to gather and food to organise. This was certainly no time to be idle.

The sun was low in the sky as Margaret prepared a meal for Archibald and their fellow tenant, John McInnes, who spent most of his day sitting in the rocking chair beside the stove. Once in a while he would walk out into the back yard and leaning on a stout stick, pull a few weeds from the vegetable garden.

The two men liked to sit by the stove and chat as Margaret prepared their food, and old John often said how lucky he was to have the McDonalds sharing his cottage. "My own family left these shores many years ago. In fact, my son Donald was one of the first to leave for the new colony of Canada and I have seven grandchildren I will never set eyes on."

Margaret thought how sad it would be if Chirsty or Catherine left and took their children with them. She was not sure she would ever forgive them if they deprived her of her grandchildren. But she cast these bleak thoughts aside and made cheery conversation as they sat down to the lobster stew and crusty bread on the table.

# Chapter 12

With the lambing season upon them, Alexander had spent little time down on the flat land where the cows grazed and the new love of his life, Sally Lamont worked in the dairy shed.

Now that his family had left the island of Ulva he had no place to visit although he had come across a number of the people still struggling to survive at Ardglass as they searched for food along the seashore or gathered wood to keep their fires burning.

High on the hillside, he spent many hours contemplating his future in far away New Zealand. Unlike, his brother's wife to be, he was sure that Sally would be willing to take her chances in the new land.

After visiting the old church and thinking about getting married there he had enticed Sally to walk up the mossy track and taken her inside the sturdy walls, just a short walk from their dwellings on the property of Francis Clark. No services were held here these days. The place felt damp and the door squeaked when it opened. But most of his family had been baptised here and Sally admitted that her christening had been carried out here as well.

"But I've never set foot inside these doors since the minister left. It's as though the ghosts are out tonight." She shivered and he put his arms around her waist. "Then wouldn't it be a good thing to let the ghosts rest in peace. Sally, will you marry me?"

Sally turned to face him and her face was alight with joy. "I thought you'd never ask, my Alex. Of course I would want to be your wife." They hugged each other in the dim light which came through the window.

"Then there is no time to waste. I'm sure that our employer would be only too happy to help us get the church ready and we will bring our families back to Ulva for the occasion." Alexander had never felt so happy. He was to be wed and soon they would be sailing off in the great ship to New Zealand.

******************

The wedding plans for Hugh and Mary were also going ahead as planned. However, Hugh felt none of his brother's confidence in the future that lay ahead. He was still filled with the desire to travel to New Zealand and the papers lay hidden in his room.

Mary was organising all the details and had borrowed a soft wool wedding gown from one of her friends who had been married the previous year. It was stored away in a cupboard and she couldn't resist bringing it out and admiring it almost every day. She was so busy with the preparations that she barely noticed that Hugh seemed less than enthusiastic.

"We now have 40 guests to feed after the wedding," she said as they strolled along the rough wooden pier at Salen. "We are so lucky that we can use the dining room at the inn and Mr McGregor says he will help meet the cost."

"You are very lucky to have such a generous employer, my dear. We would be struggling to feed so many without the help of friends and family. And we also must consider where we are to live after the wedding." With the idea of going to New Zealand still occupying his mind, Hugh had given little thought to finding accommodation.

The small hut he occupied on the farm where he worked would hardly do, especially as he shared it with two others. They would probably be welcome at Mary's parents' cottage in Salen, but she had several brothers and sisters who filled the rooms.

"We can go on living at the inn, I'm sure," Mary smiled. But the idea of living in such boisterous surroundings did not appeal to Hugh, who loved the peace and quiet of the countryside. He wouldn't be happy living in the village of Salen, especially at the noisy inn. He knew he would have to talk to Mary about New Zealand but he didn't want to spoil her happiness with the wedding coming up so soon.

It wasn't often that the two brothers had the chance to meet but the opportunity came when, by coincidence, they both visited their parents in Tobermory on the same day. Hugh was surprised to see Alexander sitting in the Argyll Terrace cottage when he walked in unannounced.

"What a treat to have both my sons here at the same time. Sit yourself down, young Hugh and share a pot of tea with us." Margaret bustled around finding another cup and Hugh sat at the table beside his brother. Their father was out on the lobster boat and was not due back until the turn of the tide and old John McInnes was out visiting a friend.

Alexander was keen to share the news of his marriage to Sally and the time passed quickly as the two men talked of their wedding plans. "We will be wed the day after Hugh and Mary," said Alexander. "We will need to make arrangements to get everyone over to Ulva for the event."

His mother thought it would have been easier to hold the ceremony in Tobermory, but she listened to her son's plans and was happy that he had finally found a young woman to share his life. Imagine, two weddings in two days. Now that was cause for celebration.

The two brothers walked down the steep incline to the jetty as Alexander planned to take the next boat back to Ulva and Hugh was to meet a friend who was driving back to Salen in a horse and cart.

"Have you thought any more about the ship to New Zealand?" Alexander asked, as soon as they were alone. "I haven't told our mother of our plans as yet. I feel it is best to wait until after the weddings."

"I think of little else, but I have been loathe to upset Mary so close to the wedding day," Hugh admitted. "I realise it may be too late if I don't get the paperwork underway soon. Has Sally agreed to go with you if you are lucky enough to be accepted?"

"I think Sally would follow me to the moon at present. She is tired of her life as a dairymaid on Ulva and wants to see more of the world I feel. I have already visited the agent and Francis Clark is also assisting us with our application."

In fact, Alexander's preparations were well advanced. With Francis Clark's help, he and Sally had filled in the necessary papers and were now anxiously awaiting confirmation that they had been accepted as assisted immigrants.

"There is less than two months to go so don't delay your decision too long," he advised his brother as they said their farewells in the street beside the jetty. "Perhaps we should let my Sally talk to Mary and see if she can influence her in any way. If she knows that she won't be alone in

the new land, it may help her to accept the idea
and be less fearful about the future."

# Chapter 13

After talking to his brother in Tobermory, Hugh caught up with his friend and was lucky to get a ride back to Salen. It would have been a long walk otherwise. His friend was feeling quite elated as he had sold a number of cattle to be taken to the mainland.

But Hugh was in no mood for talking. He was to be married in just over a month's time to a girl he loved but who was unwilling to follow him on his dream journey to New Zealand. He really had to get the issue sorted or he might miss the chance to be on the boat that would take many of the people from Mull to a new life filled with promise.

Maybe Alexander's wife-to-be Sally would be the best person to consult with. She would hopefully convince his Mary that there would be a good life on the other side of the world. As Hugh returned to his small dwelling on the hillside above Salen he knew that there was no future there for him.

Imagine owning 20 acres of land with funds to build a house. And work guaranteed in the new colony. There was no way he could ever own such a property on the small Scottish island of Mull.

The shadows on the land formed a picture in his mind. He could see the hills and plains of the new land as clearly as if he was there. He could imagine he and his brother building their crude houses from the wood that grew on their land and the stock feeding on the pastures once the bush was cleared.

He fell into a restless sleep and still the images crowded his mind. He woke and walked outside the hut to chase away the thoughts. Once the wedding was over he had to convince his bride that the only future for them was in that far-off place.

The sun was rising over the hills as he returned to his shelter and pulled on a coat ready for the morning's work. He cut a hunk of bread from a loaf on the table and added a slice of cheese. That would be sufficient to fill him until the mid-day meal which he would share with the other farm servants.

The course, stubbly grass was steaming in the early morning sun and once in a while he could see the distant bay where he knew his father Archibald would be out on the early lobster run. The old man seemed to be settling well into his new life in Tobermory, even though he had been so determined to live out his days on Ulva. If his father could make the change, surely Mary would eventually come around to his way of thinking.

*******************

Mary McKinnon was busy in the warm kitchen at the inn in Salen. She had put a large pot of porridge on the stove to heat and was stirring it with a long wooden ladle. There were a number of hungry guests to feed and soon the oat cakes would be ready to take out of the oven.

She thought of her meeting with Hugh the day before and how unwilling he was to discuss their plans for life after the wedding. "I hope Hugh hasn't changed his mind about marrying me," she confided to Annie, the cook, who was setting out the trays ready to be taken to the bedrooms.

"Of course not, my dear. All men are the same. They begin to feel trapped once they have a wife to look after. It took me all my time to get my Charlie down the aisle." She laughed heartily at the memory of their wedding a few months back. "No, he's set his heart on marrying you and he's a good man and will not go back on his word."

As soon as the breakfast had been served and the pots and plates washed and dried, Mary was free to go back to the room she shared with Annie at the back of the inn. Where would she and Hugh be sleeping once they were wed? She shivered in anticipation. So far, they had done little more than cuddle and kiss, and the prospect of going any further than that was one she daren't think about.

She knew the act of love could lead to a bairn and she wasn't sure she was ready for that prospect right now. No, all she could think about was the wedding in the church and the feast that would follow in the dining room at the inn.

She pulled out the soft wool dress once more and tried the short lace veil that her mother had worn on her wedding day. There would be flowers in her hair and she planned to carry a small bouquet picked from the garden outside the inn.

A pair of soft leather slippers lay in the box beside the dress. Hugh's brother-in-law Donald McArthur had made them for his wife Chirsty when they were wed and they had only been worn one more time when Hugh's sister Catherine married Neil MacLougas a short time later.

They were a size too small for Mary, but she knew she would just be wearing them for a short time and then change into her comfortable shoes once she got back to the inn. Reluctantly she packed away the dress and slippers, and pulled a shawl on over her dress ready to go outdoors.

As she walked between the row of tidy cottages, Mary dreamed of living in one of them some day. A few agricultural workers lived in the poorer houses, but most of the cottages built by Lachlan

81

MacQuarrie still housed tradesmen, including a tailor, shoemaker, turner, wheelwright and weaver.

John Macintyre, a merchant ship agent, lived in the grandest building at the end of the road close to the pier. Beside him was the house of the sheriff officer Donald MacLean, and the schoolmaster Thomas Duff lived in the same cluster of dwellings. The inn was at the far end of the village on the road to Gruline, almost opposite the church.

As Mary passed the church, she saw the lean figure of the minister, Mungo Campbell, walking towards the gate that led to his house. He stopped when he saw Mary and waited until she came closer.

"Mistress McKinnon, it's a pleasure to see you. How are all your plans coming along?" He leaned on the wooden gate as if ready for a long conversation. "It's time that you and your young man came by to visit me before the Banns are read in the church."

Mary blushed and muttered her reply. She had been trying to make a time for Hugh to accompany her to this meeting with the minister, but he had always found a reason not to attend. Once again she felt uneasy. Surely Hugh was not having a change of heart about the marriage.

Perhaps the idea of sailing to New Zealand was still on his mind and he was trying to decide where his future lay. Oh, why did things have to become so complicated right now when it should be the happiest time of her life?

She returned to the inn where the warmth and sound of laughter welcomed her. She loved the busy atmosphere and the cheerful talk as the men enjoyed a companionable drink around the roaring fire. She would miss her work if she ever had to live in a different place.

No, a solitary dwelling high on the hillside or in a dreary little bay was not her idea of living. She needed the company of people and a bustling village atmosphere. If she had her way, Hugh would soon be living with her in Salen and she could continue working at the inn amongst her friends.

## Chapter 14

It was a warm, sunny morning and Donald was busy out in the back house where he was making a set of boots for an order which would go over on the boat to Oban as soon as it was completed.

Margaret had taken young John and Archibald out walking, leaving Chirsty with instructions to rest. She clasped her arms protectively around her belly. Yes, this baby was going to be born alive and well, she was sure.

Feeling restless, she walked along the narrow lane between the stone cottages and soon came to the lookout at the end of Argyll Terrace where someone had erected a wooden seat, from where a magnificent view over Tobermory Bay could be enjoyed.

The older children were in school and the girls in particular were busy practising their items for the upcoming Ceilidh. They were anxious to please their new teacher who knew there would be strong competition from the visiting children.

Chirsty sat and took in the view and thought about her father Archibald McDonald who was settling into life in Tobermory, although at his age, working on the lobster boats was probably too strenuous. But the younger lads looked after him, knowing his experience and skill meant a lot more than brute strength at times.

Yes, those were the days on Ulva when she had had the time to help her father bring the lobsters from the creels onto the small boat and how good money was made from their sale, especially when the inn was going at full strength, and buying all they could supply.

As she passed the school building she could hear the sound of fiddles practising their item for the big event. She knew that young Ketty would be earnestly concentrating on the notes, although sometimes the sound didn't come out exactly as she wanted.

Back at the cottage she stopped to talk to Donald in his workshop. He held up the boots for her inspection. They were made from strong leather and would last for many a day, she knew.

"It's a fine day, my dear," Donald paused in his work to look at his wife. "And you are looking bonny as well." He smiled, confident that his time they would have a healthy child to add to their family.

"Yes, Donald. And when this new bairn arrives I will name him for you," Chirsty promised. They put their arms around each other, taking the rare chance to be together without the prying eyes of their children. Then Chirsty pulled away, and backed out of the small space.

"Now I must go and collect the children from your mother. Old Margaret should not be burdened with them when I am well enough to do the job." But Chirsty felt light-hearted as she left, knowing her husband's love for her was strong. Yes, she had chosen well when she wed her neighbour, Donald McArthur, all those years ago on Ulva.

Margaret McDonald was pleased to see Chirsty looking so bonny with her cheeks flushed pink from the fresh salty air. "I'm to meet with young Hugh and Mary tomorrow to discuss their wedding plans. I will ride over to Salen on the early mail cart and stay overnight at the inn."

Chirsty found it hard to believe that both her brothers were to be married soon and hoped she would be well enough to attend, one wedding in Salen and the other on the island of Ulva. It would certainly be a time of celebration for the family, though Donald had hinted that the lads were thinking of going off in the big ship to New Zealand. That would be hard for their mother who obviously hadn't yet heard the rumour.

Mind you, half the young men in town were thinking of joining the ship and some had already been accepted as immigrants in the new country. They were filled with excitement at the thought of the land on offer and the chance to build a house in the bush.

Donald had warned her of trouble with the native people in the north who were losing their land to the new arrivals. Most were friendly but a few were protesting at the new developments on their shores. There was talk of an uprising even though a treaty had been signed many years before.

She didn't mention anything about New Zealand to her mother. It would be sad to spoil her excitement at the idea of two of her sons being wed. "They are such charming young women. Mary being so full of life, and Sally so strong. I fear she will be a handful for our Alexander to tame."

The women laughed at the thought. The children came bursting through the door at that moment, full of news of the day's events. "I'm to sing by myself at the Ceilidh," Ketty proudly announced. "No, you ain't, you're singing with the rest of us," her brother argued.

"But the teacher asked me to sing by myself," Ketty wailed. She was envious of her cousin Sarah whose singing was to be one of the highlights, according to their grandmother. There were just two weeks left until the children from the small school were to arrive for the big event.

The 10 children were all to stay in the school for two nights and enough bedding and food had been promised to accommodate them. Margaret had been busy with the arrangements but now felt she could spare a day to visit her youngest son in Salen. "Well, I'll be off home now," she said. "It'll soon be time to prepare a meal for Archibald and old John."

Chirsty smiled as she watched her mother leave. She was certainly settling very well into life in Tobermory. In fact, it was the best thing to have happened to both families, with Donald so busy with his shoemaking and the children happily settled into their school.

Her own life was a busy one but she was content and happily setting up the small cradle and coverings for the new bairn, who would sleep in the same room as she and Donald for the first few months. The other children all shared the two large rooms up the stairs which were now looking homely with their wooden beds and bright coloured quilts. She and Margaret had hung curtains at the windows and the dwelling was a far cry from the stone hut they had occupied on the smaller island of Ulva.

Over the meal of broth and bread, Chirsty told Donald of her mother's proposed visit to Salen the next day. "She is sure to take the time to visit the grave of her sister Ann and old John Curry," she said.

"Aye, it seems that our children are learning their lessons quickly even after the lack of schooling on Ulva. Thanks to your mother, and the education she received from John Curry, they haven't been left too far behind." Donald always felt that the scholarly ways of their children came from Chirsty's side of the family rather than his own. He had struggled with book learning and had taken up shoemaking at an early age.

As the last rays of sunlight shone through the flimsy curtains the pair sat together in contented silence, only broken by the return of the children who had been playing with their friends in the street behind the cottage.

Little Archibald was dusty from rolling in the grass and the girls were admonishing their brother John for encouraging his antics. "He'll have to be washed again before he goes to bed," said Ketty, who knew she would probably get the job.

"Never mind, it won't take a moment." Chirsty was calm as she rinsed a cloth in the pot of hot water beside the fireplace and soon had her youngest son looking clean and rather pink from the warmth. "Now off with you to bed and your father will tell you a story of the early days on Ulva when we lived in a leaky, smoky cottage and ate potatoes and dried herrings for our supper."

# Chapter 15

Hugh had just returned to his humble dwelling when he found a note from his mother to say she was visiting the next day and would meet him at the inn after work.

He was pleased to have the chance to talk about the wedding plans but felt a pang of guilt that he had not yet told her of his hopes to travel to New Zealand with his new bride.   In fact, he had not even broached the subject with Mary as he knew there would be tears and possible tantrums if she knew what he was planning. She and her mother, as well as her sister, could think of nothing else but the wedding day and were busy making all the necessary arrangements.

"It will be the most beautiful day possible," she had said dreamily when they last walked along the windy pier at Salen. "My sister will be wearing a borrowed gown. And as for me?" She blushed and giggled. "You will have to wait and see."

The inn-keeper had made a generous offer to supply meats and bread and Mary's mother and her friends were planning to bake a variety of small goods. Margaret and Donald would supply a modest amount of alcohol and the afternoon would be a lively one following the traditional marriage ceremony at the Salen Church.

Hugh looked around the small hut he shared with two other lads and thought of the chance to own land and a dwelling in New Zealand. He knew he would be living near the southern city of Dunedin which had been settled by Scots a few years earlier.

There was even the prospect of finding gold in the nearby rivers while he was waiting for the trees on his land to be felled and grass and crops planted. The only problem he could envisage was persuading his new wife to leave her family and accompany him.

*******************

It was barely light when Margaret McDonald stood outside the town hall on Tobermory's main street to wait for the mail cart that would take her to Salen. It would be a long, slow journey as the cart would stop at a number of small settlements to drop off the bags of letters and packages and other supplies.

She would probably have the chance to visit the grave of her father John Curry and sister Ann as they passed the cemetery at Pennygown, and view the fine monument erected by Ann's husband John MacDonald the joiner.

By the time the mail carrier had loaded the cart and hoisted Margaret aboard, they were off at a brisk pace, the sturdy pony trotting along the dusty road and covering the miles much more quickly than Margaret could have imagined.

It wasn't long before they stopped at Ardnacross and caught a glimpse of the last remaining standing stone upright in the field. It was here at Ardnacross that Donald McDonald had been born and Margaret's life had begun at Scallastle just a few miles further down the coast where the Curry family had lived.

Soon the ruins of Aros Castle, once the home of the MacDonalds, came into view. The castle had been built more than 600 years earlier and not much remained of its fearsome might.

Margaret was beginning to tire as Salen Bay came into view, with the familiar line of stone cottages and mail office in the middle of the town. From there it was a short walk to the inn on the busy corner where the road divided and crossed a narrow strip of land to the western shore.

A feeling of sadness came over her as Margaret passed the tidy dwelling where her sister Ann had lived until her death a few short years before. Even while living on Ulva, Margaret had brought her children across on the boat and stayed in Salen and the two had spent many happy hours together. Charles was the only one of Ann's children still living in the town and with any luck she would catch him late in the evening. He and his wife Susan still lived in Ann's old cottage but did not have children so the couple worked together out on the hillsides with the sheep and cattle.

But now it was time to greet her future daughter-in-law and young Mary was all smiles as Margaret walked into the inn which was crowded with noisy drinkers from the wharf site. The two embraced and Margaret was shown the small upstairs room that she had rented for the night. A narrow bed took up most of the space and a wooden cupboard stood in the corner.

"Well, Mary. How are your wedding plans coming along?" Margaret was eager to catch up with all the news and they spent the next few minutes talking before Mary returned to her work in the busy kitchen.

As it was still early afternoon Margaret decided to walk across the road and into the church where Hugh and Mary were to be married. The sombre stone building held a host of memories and as she entered she could feel the spirits of all the dead crowding around her. There had been exciting times too, with the opening of the church which had been a big occasion for her brother-in-law John MacDonald, who had crafted the fittings and solid wooden seats.

Sitting in the pew where her sister Ann had once worshipped, Margaret recalled christenings and funerals, and the wedding of her son Hugh and his bride Mary McKinnon would be a welcome occasion for all the family.

By the time she returned to the inn, it was time to relax beside the roaring fire and enjoy a mug of beer until the meal was ready. Hugh arrived just as the food was to be served so there was little time for talk as they piled their plates with beef, vegetables and slabs of bread and sat down at the long table.

Margaret thought her son looked a little thin and worn but made no comment. He must be working hard to save for the wedding. Hugh was curious about the forthcoming marriage of his brother Alexander and Sally Lamont. It would not be as grand as the wedding Mary was planning, but would mean a lot to the family to revisit the small church on Ulva. He was beginning to wish that he was being married there as well. All this talk of weddings was for the womenfolk.

It wasn't until they reached the subject of where they would live, that Margaret noticed his reluctance to continue the conversation. "We haven't quite decided yet," stammered Hugh, at the same time as Mary answered that there was an available room attached to the inn. It was obvious that the living arrangements were yet to be sorted.

But Mary was oblivious to the problem and chatted on about gowns and flowers and shoes and music while Hugh sat silently staring at the flames. After a time, when Mary was busy clearing the table and taking the dishes into the scullery to be washed, Margaret had a chance to question her son.

"Hugh, you seem a little distracted. Is everything alright between yourself and Mary? She's a bonny lass but a bit of a town body. Not well suited to life on the land I would say."

"Aye, mother. That's the way it is. My Mary likes her security and is loathe to venture far from her family. But I fancy her and want her for my wife."

"Just be patient and it will work itself out," suggested Margaret. "She is young and has never travelled far from her home. She will make you a fine, caring wife and a good mother when the time comes I am sure."

The thought of more grandchildren to come filled her heart with delight, and hopefully sons to carry on the McDonald name.

Hugh left shortly after the meal, promising to catch up with his mother next time he visited Tobermory. He would need to meet the officials from the emigration office who were recruiting prospects for the journey to New Zealand. But there were many decisions to be made before then.

Would he be able to talk Mary into accepting the idea? Should he tell her his plans before or after the wedding?

# Chapter 16

The sun shone down onto the grassy bank where Alexander lay with Sally, his bride to be. Their love making had taken on a new urgency and it was only at the last moment that Donald reluctantly pulled away, his frustration building.

Sally was loathe to stop, but he was determined to wait until their wedding night, and maybe longer, as the sea journey to New Zealand would be difficult enough without the possibility of an ailing and pregnant wife.

"Sally, my love, there will be time enough for love making once we are in the fine new land." Alexander lifted Sally to her feet and they hastily straightened their clothing before making their way down the hill to the Ulva Church where their wedding would take place.

"It's time we made some arrangements." Sally pulled herself together reluctantly to talk of practical things. "Most of your family will be staying over night in Salen after Hugh's marriage. We must decide how they will travel from there to Ulva in time for our wedding the next day."

Alexander realised that he had thought little about the wedding plans, his mind so occupied with the voyage to New Zealand and the new life ahead. "You are right, my dear. We will need to arrange transport to bring them from Salen to the Ulva ferry. I'm sure my employer, Francis Clark, will be willing to help us out. He has been so helpful already in booking our passage on the ship and signing all the documents on our behalf."

The little stone church stood before them, the walls covered in green moss and the gateway hanging from a broken bolt. The unlocked door creaked as Alexander pushed it open and a musty smell hit them as they cautiously entered.

With most of the tenants gone from the island, the church was rarely used these days so it would take an army of cleaners to prepare the building for the wedding ceremony. And would the visiting preacher be prepared to come over to this remote place?

But Sally could see the possibilities and her mind was set on being married here. A shaft of sunlight gleamed on the old wooden alter and the solid pews could be easily cleaned and polished. She would bring over soap and cleaning cloths and enlist the help of her friends from mansion house.

"A few garlands of bracken and flowers will make all the difference and, of course, I'll have to find a dress to wear," she enthused. "The church is so close to the mansion and this will give us something to do on our days off to make the time go more quickly."

Alexander laughed as they closed the door and walked hand in hand back to Ulva House. Sally was so filled with joy and optimism. Their wedding day would be a magic occasion.

************************

While Alexander was eagerly looking forward to his marriage to Sally, Hugh was having trouble envisaging his future. He was anxious to make Mary his wife, but all this talk of weddings and no discussion of life afterwards was making him increasingly nervous.

Although the couple often walked together, it was rare for them to be alone. There were usually others standing outside their cottages, or fishing from the pier, and the inn was always noisy and crowded. "I would like to be alone with you some time, my Mary." Hugh was beginning to get frustrated at the lack of privacy. "Why not come with me out into the fields with just the sky above us and a few sheep for company?"

But Mary just laughed and carried on walking along the dusty road. She was nervous at the thought of being alone with Hugh, and had so far discouraged any attempts at intimacy. A quick kiss was all she would allow.

She turned and smiled at him now. "Come on, Hugh. Let's not talk of serious matters. There is a lifetime ahead of us for that. But we do need to discuss the problem of getting your family from Salen to Ulva for Alexander's wedding. I wish they would just get married here in Salen immediately after us."

Hugh agreed that would be simple solution but knew that Alexander and Sally were keen to have their own ceremony on the island where they were born, with as little fuss as possible. Once again he reluctantly listened to Mary as she reeled off the endless lists of people who they should invite to the church ceremony and the feast at the inn to follow.

Back at the inn he was urged to remain for a while and take a quick whisky before heading back to the hillside croft. Mary was the centre of attention as she poured the ale into stout mugs and handed them out to the men and women gathered in the cosy room. She was so happy in her own world. Was he wrong to want her to live in a far-off, foreign place?

She gave Hugh a wave as he left the room and he was soon walking along the dusty track that led up the hill to the farmland. Once again, no future plans had been discussed and time was running out if he wanted to be on the ship to New Zealand.

******************

With the weddings and the upcoming musical celebration almost upon them, Margaret McDonald was busier that ever spinning yarn and organising garments for the children to wear. The school children would all be dressed in white shirts and dark skirts or trousers, but would wear colourful dyed sashes to distinguish one group from another.

The Tobermory children were to wear green and the children from the visiting school would be supplied with bright red sashes on the day of the concert. A number of pupils from Salen and smaller schools dotted along the rugged coastline would also be taking part, but would be returning to their settlements at the end of the day.

"I'm sure there are not enough hours in the day for all that has to be done." Margaret pulled a steaming pile of dyed wool from the large pot over the outdoor fire, and flung it across the wooden fence to dry in the sun.

"That is a fine colour. The berries we gathered have proved to be useful after all," said Chirsty, who was helping out as best she could. Her face sweated from the heat of the fire and her legs ached.

"Go sit yourself down my girl, and leave the work to me." Margaret scolded her daughter. "There'll be enough for you to do soon with a new child to care for."

Old Archibald was sitting on an upturned box and laughed at his wife's bossiness. He was used to Margaret and her energetic ways. "Best do as your mother says, lass. She has a way of making you toe the line as we all well know."

Chirsty was only too pleased to do as her mother said and rest for the moment. She knew that her hands would be full once the new baby was born.

Her elder son John had recently started attending the school along with his sisters, and there was only young Archibald left at home during the day. He was a good child and content to watch his father in the shoemaker's hut or spend time with his grandparents next door.

She thought for a moment about the dead baby she had held a short time ago, but was confident that soon they would all be celebrating the birth of a strong, healthy child.

# Chapter 17

With just weeks to go before her wedding day, Sally Lamont felt suddenly overwhelmed with the number of tasks to be carried out to prepare for the big event.

Like Alexander, her thoughts had been more on the excitement of the move to New Zealand than anything else, but now she needed to take some time out for herself. Her employer Francis Clark was happy to allow her a few days off from the dairy shed and she thought it would be a good chance to visit Alexander's folks and get to know them a little better.

"I'll pay a visit to your parents in Tobermory, then call in to see Hugh's Mary at Salen on my way back and learn more about their plans," she told Alexander over the evening meal they shared with the other farm workers.

"Be careful not to mention the ship to New Zealand," Alexander warned. "I haven't yet told my parents and I don't think Hugh has discussed the possibility any further with Mary."

Sally felt a stab of impatience. "You will have to let them all know very soon. The word is sure to get out with so many signed up for the voyage and our names already on the list."

Alexander agreed and knew his brother would have to make a decision soon. There were few places left on the great ship which would soon leave the Tobermory shores. It was a unique opportunity as most of the ships left from the port of Clyde which added several days onto the journey.

"Take care, my lass, and enjoy your visit. It's a long while since you left the island and ventured into town. Maybe my mother and sister could help you find a dress to wear on your wedding day and you will need clothing to take to New Zealand soon after. Goodness only knows what will be available in that far-off place."

So, Sally left next day on a small fishing craft which would take her around the northern shores of the island of Mull right to the town of Tobermory. She carried a small bundle of over-night clothing and a purse full of cash that she had been saving for many months.

The rugged coastline was unfamiliar to Sally as she had not travelled this way before. The few times she had visited Mull she had taken the road to Salen, then along the eastern side of the island to Tobermory. The fishermen were in a relaxed mood as they were delivering a boatful of herrings to the town and staying in the port overnight.

"It's a fine day for an outing," a cheery lad ventured. "And what would be taking you to Tobermory?" Sally smiled as she answered boldly. "I'm to find a dress for my wedding and visit with my future family."

She went on to talk about the McDonalds and how they would soon be her kinsfolk. It was the first time she had talked to anyone outside her fellow workers and it brought a throb of excitement to her voice. Before she knew it she was sharing the dream of living in New Zealand with all the fishermen and there was envy in their eyes as they listened to her words.

By the time they moored at the Tobermory jetty, Sally was sure that half the men on board would be putting their names on the list to sail to the new colony. With enthusiasm mounting she climbed the steep track to the upper village where she knew she would be welcomed by Margaret McDonald and her family. As Sally passed the school yard she heard the sound of singing, and stopped to listen to the children as they practised their items for the Ceilidh.

Soon she was on the narrow lane behind Donald and Chirsty's house and caught sight of the shoemaker hard at work in the back house. She had not seen Donald since he and the family had left Ulva to live on Mull and she felt a little shy as she approached him. But his welcome was a friendly one as he laid down his tools and took her into the house to find his wife.

Sally could scarcely believe the difference in the family's living conditions. The desolate little dwelling on Ulva was a world away from this solid little cottage with its cheery fire and

105

cooking stove. She could see the steps leading up into the attic rooms where the children slept and dreamed for a moment that this would be the sort of home that she and Alexander would build some day.

Chirsty rose from her seat by the fireplace and put her arms around Sally. "What a pleasant surprise. Our mother will be most happy to see you and learn about your wedding plans." In fact, at that moment Margaret came bustling into the room, her arms full of the yarn that was now dry and ready to weave.

She was delighted to see her future daughter-in-law and Donald smiled as he returned to his work, leaving the women to catch up with all the news. It would be good for Chirsty to take her mind off her pregnancy.

The day passed quickly as Margaret took in the situation regarding the wedding plans, or lack of them, and she soon came up with a suggestion about a dress for Sally. She remembered that her friend Mary McNeil had kept the wedding gown that her daughter had worn before leaving to live in Glasgow. She was sure that there would be no objection to Sally borrowing the dress and it could be altered to fit.

Transporting the family from Salen to Ulva for the wedding, however, would be a more difficult problem to solve.

"I'm sure we will work it out and there is plenty of room at the Mansion House." Sally was confident that her employer would offer accommodation for the family.

The subject was left there as the children chose that moment to arrive back from school. Little Archibald woke from his sleep and with the three older children crowding into the room it was soon obvious that talk of wedding arrangements would have to wait. As her family crowded into the small cottage Chirsty wondered how she had ever coped in the cramped conditions back on Ulva.

The elderly lodger, John McInnes, had now been moved into the Poor House, so the two girls were sleeping with Margaret and Archibald next door. Now, with the boys in the attic room, there would be space for the new child once he was old enough to be away from his mother. Chirsty always thought of the baby as a boy, and was determined to name him Donald after his father.

With a spare room up the stairs, Sally was welcomed to stay as many nights as she wished which would give her ample opportunity to get to know her new family. What a time she was having. Life with Alexander would definitely be a varied and exciting one.

# Chapter 18

While Sally was busily working on her wedding plans with Alexander's family at Tobermory, Mary McKinnon was growing anxious about the lack of answers about their life after her wedding to Hugh. Whenever she brought up the subject about where they would live, Hugh managed to avoid answering.

Mary was certain that Hugh still loved her, but he seemed reluctant to discuss the wedding or their future plans once they were married. She hoped that he wasn't still considering the move to New Zealand. The thought of that long voyage and a life so far from all her familiar surroundings filled her with dread.

She busied herself in the dining room, clearing away the remnants of lunch and carrying the dishes back to the washing tub in the large kitchen. It was best to keep busy when these things were playing on her mind.

They would be perfectly comfortable in the small room on offer at the back of the inn and it would do nicely until a suitable dwelling could be found for them. Hugh would need to stay away during the busy lambing season but that was the way of all the farmhands. They slept out in the rough shelters on the hillsides when there was work to be done.

Why did life have to be so uncertain when the answers were so simple? Her friend Annie noticed her silence and commented: "Is something troubling you, Mary? You are not your usual cheery self."

"It's just that men folk don't seem to understand the ways of women. Hugh won't talk about our wedding or where we will live as husband and wife." Mary wrung out the dish cloth and washed down the soapy wooden bench.

"He's obviously leaving all the arrangements up to you, my dear. I'm sure he will be more than happy to fit in with your plans." Annie stacked the dishes on a shelf as she tried to reassure her friend. "He will be more than agreeable to bed down with you once the day is over." She smiled at memories of her own wedding night a short time ago.

Mary blushed and stammered as she tried to change the subject. That part of the marriage was something she was not too sure about and she was not about to discuss such an intimate subject with anyone. It was all so difficult. Did every young bride feel so unsure of her future? She did feel stirrings when she and Hugh were close but always rebuffed him when he tried to go further.

Once her chores were finished, Mary returned to her room and brought out the box with her wedding gown and shoes. She held the dress up against her slim body and did a little dance around the bed. "Only a few weeks to go," she said to herself, and let out a little sigh. She enjoyed her work at the busy inn and would continue to serve the customers and clean up the dishes for as long as she was able. Maybe until she was with child, and  hopefully, by then, she and Hugh would surely have a small place of their own.


******************

Back in Tobermory, Sally was kept busy helping Chirsty with the children and assisting with the arrangements at the school. Only a week to go before the big event and everyone was excited at the prospect of hosting the visiting children in their village. Margaret was looking forward to seeing her grandchildren, especially young Sarah who would be leading the singing.

Chirsty was in safe hands as the old doctor had recommended a good midwife and he would be close by if needed. Her thoughts still went back to the tiny baby girl who had been born such a short time ago on Ulva, but was sure she carried a healthy child this time.

She busied herself sorting the coloured sashes the children would be wearing at the Ceilidh. Sally had taken the little ones for a walk down to the jetty and the others were practising their songs at the school. Donald was visiting the distant island of Iona with an order of boots and shoes so it was good to be alone for a time.

She was tempted to climb the steep steps up to the attic room where the older children slept but had promised Donald that she wouldn't take the risk until after the birth of their child. The wooden cradle was ready for the new bairn and she folded and unfolded the soft woollen blanket that her mother had woven.

The sound of excited voices brought her back to the present with a jolt and she moved the kettle of water to the middle of the stove to prepare a hot drink for the children. Sally was with them and almost as excited as the children. "They are doing so well with their singing and the fiddle playing is something to smile about." She grimaced a little at the thought of 12 children all scraping their fiddles at the same time. But their enthusiasm was contagious.

Chirsty was happy to have the company of her bright new friend and was sure her brother had chosen his spouse well. She was bonny enough too, although a little on the heavy side, but her cheery nature was infectious. She instructed the girls to climb the steps and straighten their bed linen, then brewed the tea and set out some oat cakes on the slab table.

"Come and sit yourself down Sally, and tell me about the music. Unfortunately I haven't ventured up to the school for a few days. Our mother Margaret is spending much of her time there as well as down in the lower village persuading the store keepers to supply food and drink for the visiting children."

The big event was to be held in the hall down near the pier and a large crowd from all over the island of Mull was expected to attend. Adults and children alike would be competing for the prizes and some fine talent would be on display. The annual Ceilidh was indeed the highlight of the year.

On the day leading up to the Ceilidh, boat races were always held in Tobermory Bay adding to the excitement of the occasion. People would travel on the ferry from Oban and spend the day watching the activities in the bay then many would remain to enjoy the feast of music at the hall.

The shop fronts were decorated for the occasion with flags and bunting. Store owners also took the opportunity to display goods to catch the eye of the hundreds of visitors. As Margaret McDonald went from store to store to seek support for feeding the school children she was caught up in the atmosphere. This was far more exciting than living on Ulva where most of the day was spent trying to keep the stone cottage warm and dry.

Even old Archibald who had been so reluctant to leave his precious island seemed to have settled well into this new life. As she passed the shipping office she saw a line of men outside the door. No doubt they were signing up to leave on the great ship and take up the promise of land and a new life on the other side of the world.

She sighed as she thought of her beloved children and hoped that none of them were planning to leave. Young Alexander had been rather secretive about the future, and as for Hugh, it was hard to tell what was going through his mind.

Several of her Curry family had left the shores of Scotland several years before and were now flourishing in Canada. She would have to encourage her sons if they were seeking a better life, but please don't let the bairns leave these shores.

With her basket full of supplies and much more promised before the weekend, Margaret knew that the visiting children would be well fed. Blankets and sleeping mattresses were already stored at the school in readiness, along with enough plates and cutlery to feed an army.

She knew that back at the isolated school room on the other side of the island preparations would be well underway. In fact, Angus McLean, the school master was spending many hours rehearsing the simple songs and dances which his pupils would perform.

They were word perfect and the final number would be 'Wind Song'.  In his heart, Angus was hoping to find a rising star and the most likely was young Sarah Maclougas who would perform the verses of the song. Hopefully his pupils would not be overwhelmed by the occasion. Several of them had never been as far as Tobermory, even though it was just a short boat trip away.

As he packed his violin into its case he watched the children run and skip up the hill towards their simple huts and prayed that they would have great opportunities in a changing world. What did the future hold for these unspoiled island children?


**********************

When Old Margaret returned to the Argyll Terrace cottage, Archibald was seated by the fireplace resting his weary bones. He had just returned from a day out on the lobster boat and although the heavy lifting was done by the younger men, his back was stiff from bending over the cages to sort out the lobsters which were not suitable to sell.

Only the large male lobsters would find their way into someone's cooking pot. He smiled when Margaret came towards him and beckoned for her to join him. "Sit yourself down, my Margaret,

114

and tell me about your day. I see you have been busy gathering even more supplies to feed those hungry children."

Archibald was glad that Margaret was so content with her life in Tobermory. At times he felt a little guilty that he had been so stubborn about moving from Ulva.

"Yes, my dear. The store keepers have been most generous and have promised meat, fruit, and many loaves of bread which will be delivered to the school on Friday. And of course, the women of the village will also be busy cooking all manner of food for the children."

It had been decided that a number of the Tobermory children would also sleep at the school and Chirsty's daughters were excited that they would be with their cousins who were arriving late on Friday. Ketty and Margaret were among those who had been chosen to sleep overnight in the school room and they would carry their bedding and a change of clothes across the road to the school later in the week.

Their teacher Archie Campbell was looking forward to seeing his former pupils and was most interested to see how they would perform. Hopefully they wouldn't be over awed by the crowd. But he would make sure they felt right at home when they arrived in Tobermory on Friday.

115

# Chapter 19

Back on Ulva, Alexander was helping Sally finish cleaning the milking shed. It was his day off and they planned to visit the church where they were to be married in a few short weeks. The minister from Salen had promised to take the service and he would join the guests for the meal to follow at the inn down by the ferry landing which had once been leased by the husband of Margaret McDonald's sister, before the family emigrated to Canada.

"We had some great times at the inn when my aunt lived there. They also bought most of the lobsters from old Archibald." Alexander had many good memories of the Ulva Inn.

After a satisfying breakfast, they were soon off along the mossy track that led to the old church which had been built more than 40 years ago. It had once been a busy, bustling place when many families lived on the island and worshiped there. A few shaggy Highland cattle were grazing in the yard and Alexander chased them out and closed the iron gate more firmly.

The heavy wooden door protested as they opened it but the interior was clean and dry. An ornate carved alter almost reached the ceiling, looking a little incongruous in such a simple building. Sally climbed the steps up to the pulpit and banged her hand on the top.

"Alexander McDonald, do you promise to love and obey?" she giggled. She looked around and realized the amount of work it would take to get the interior ready for a wedding, but knew the other farm workers would willingly lend a hand. Sally also had two brothers living on Ulva who could be called upon when the time came.

"If my mother still lived close by she would have been able to help us," Alexander said. "My family won't be coming over from Salen until after Hugh and Mary's wedding. We can't count on them to help too much."

"Your family is very supportive of our plans and your mother arranged for me to borrow a beautiful wedding gown." Sally smiled at the memory of her happy visit to Tobermory.

Alexander wasn't sure how many of his folks would be able to attend. Both his sisters would have young children to consider but Hugh and Mary had promised to be there. His parents were to stay at the inn following the celebrations so they would be comfortable over night. As for himself and Sally, they would have to share a small room at Ulva Mansion.

He pulled Sally down from the steps and held her for a moment. He was so happy that she had consented to be his wife and before they knew it, they would be on the ship and sailing off to New Zealand.

"I haven't spoken to my brother for some time. I hope he has made his travel arrangements. The places on the ship are filling up fast." Alexander was concerned about Hugh and whether he had persuaded Mary to leave her home and family and make the long journey across the sea.

Sally threw her arms around him and gave him a big squeeze. "You and I are going and that is all that matters. Don't be concerned about your brother. It's up to him to do what he thinks is best."

Alexander was loathe to leave Sally's warm grasp but knew that they should continue on with their walk. They planned to call at Sally's brother's cottage and tell him of their marriage plans, then spend time clearing Alexander's room ready for their wedding night.

*********************

Although she tried to rest as much as possible, Chirsty's days were busy. There were always so many hungry mouths to feed and although her mother was right next door, the tasks of keeping the cottage clean and warm seemed to fill up all her time.

"I'm sorry I haven't been to help you at the school," she said one morning as Margaret was setting off with the older children. Young Archibald was now the only child left at home during the day and he loved to watch his father at work in the shoemaker's shop.

"At least you will be able to get to the Ceilidh and hear the children sing. It promises to be a grand occasion." Margaret had heard several of the practices and knew that their enthusiasm made up for their occasional lack of pitch.

"Have you heard whether Catherine is coming with the children? I would love to see little Mary Ann again."

They hadn't heard anything from the Maclougas family but hoped that Catherine would be able to accompany her daughters and be there to hear Sarah perform.

When Margaret returned she looked around Chirsty's crowded house and wondered how she had ever managed while they were living in the small dwelling on Ulva. The two eldest girls had taken to sleeping in Archibald and Margaret's house next door and more often than not, the family ate together. They had found another boarder to take old John's place, a young lad who worked on the lobster boats, so this helped pay the rent for the cottage.

With the money Archibald earned from fishing and the little extra she brought in from the sale of her woollen scarves, they were able to put a little money aside for when Archibald was no longer able to work. The cold conditions out on the sea were affecting his arthritis and the sooner he could give up the better it would be.

But Margaret was content with her new life in Tobermory. She loved the walk down the steep track to the waterfront where the stores provided a wide variety of goods. The clatter of the wheelwright's shop and the smell of yeast coming from the brewery, the tannery where sheep and cattle hides were turned into leather and the jostle of people who crowded into the general store filled her with excitement.

She didn't regret her years raising her family on the remote island of Ulva, but was pleased her children and grandchildren would have a much more satisfying life.

# Chapter 20

After weeks of preparation the big day had come. It was time for the children to arrive with their schoolmaster to take part in the Ceilidh at the town hall the following day. Angus McLean was a little nervous as he helped the children unload their belongings at the Tobermory jetty and hoped they would not be overwhelmed, but would enjoy the experience.

He carried his precious fiddle under his arm along with a box of musical notes for the pianist who would accompany the children. He knew they would have time to practise once they arrived at the school.

Archie Campbell was at the wharf to meet the excited youngsters who were happy to see their former teacher. He was accompanied by the two eldest Macarthur children as their cousins were among the visitors and they would make them feel at home.

He knew that Margaret McDonald and several of the other parents were waiting at the school to welcome the visiting children and offer them some warm food and drink.

"This is certainly a grand occasion." He shook Archie by the hand and offered to carry the box of music. "Perhaps this could be the start of an annual visit."

Archie smiled. "It is a great opportunity for our children to show off their talents. You certainly taught them well while they were in your care."

Ketty and Margaret had caught up with their cousins and were soon chattering away as they walked through the village and up the hill to the school. It was a steep climb and they stopped once in a while to look back at the view of the bay and admire the cottages with their colourful gardens.

"Our grandmother will be waiting for us at the school. She has been so busy gathering food and bedding for everyone. We are staying over as well and it's all so exciting." Young Ketty was full of importance as she led her cousins along the cobbled road.

Sarah was quiet as she stared at the buildings and houses along the way. She kept a close eye on her two sisters, and both Catherine and Margaret were equally overwhelmed. There were 10 children from their school and they had practised their songs every day for weeks, but to perform in front of a whole village was going to be a new experience.

When the school came into view, the first person they saw was their grandmother, Margaret McDonald, who came forward with open arms to greet them. "Welcome, my darlings. We are so happy to have you here." She led the way into the building where several of the Tobermory children were waiting.

Mary McNeil was organising the women who were preparing the food and drinks and soon all the children were lining up for a cup of soup and a plate of warm oat biscuits. They were silent at first but soon their shyness was forgotten as they went off to see where they were going to sleep and sort themselves out some bedding. Straw-filled mattresses covered with a pile of coloured rugs would keep them warm and comfortable and each child placed their bundle of clothing on top of the beds before going outside to play in the school yard.

"I think they will be fine." Margaret breathed a sigh of relief as she watched the children playing together. "They will need to come inside and practise their items as soon as the pianist arrives."

A short time later the young woman who was organizing the Ceilidh arrived to meet the children and they were all herded inside for a final rehearsal. The pianist was also ready and a large pile of music was placed on top of the piano. Luckily, Agnes Brown had a good eye and was quick to master a tune.

The children were summoned indoors where rows of seats were ready. First the Tobermory children were called up and sang through their items, accompanied by the pianist. Then it was the turn of the fiddle players who managed to

keep in tune. A group of dancers was next and
then it was time for the visiting children to
perform their items.

A lively bracket of songs soon had the audience
clapping along, but then they were quiet as Angus
McLean stood and played the first notes of a
plaintive melody.

The children joined in, singing of the wind and
sea, and then it was Sarah's turn. Her voice was
clear and true and at first she sung
unaccompanied, then the violin joined in and the
people were amazed at the sound. When she
finished there was long silence and then everyone
in the room was on their feet and the applause
continued for several minutes. Old Margaret
wiped the tears from her eyes. Her young grand
daughter was sure to be the star of the show.

*********************

Back on Ulva, Alexander and Sally's wedding
plans were taking shape. Now she had borrowed
the handsome gown from Mary McNeil and a
head dress from Francis Clark's daughter, Sally
was ready for the big day.

She and Alexander had been back to the church
on several occasions, to clean and tidy the
building. The pulpit and seats were polished and
with a few flower arrangements and bundles of
fern the old building would be ready.

They had been given a large tin trunk to take to New Zealand and Sally was busy packing their belongings ready for the long sea voyage. Bed linen and blankets would take up much of the space along with sturdy boots, shoes and warm clothing.

Alexander knew that he could no longer delay telling his family that they were leaving on the great ship, so decided to visit Tobermory for the Ceilidh and inform them of his plans. He also needed to call at the shipping office to collect some papers and finalise the arrangements.

Early on Saturday morning he took the small ferry across to Mull and caught a ride in a farm cart to the village of Salen. He knew that Hugh would be away working in the fields, but decided to call at the inn to talk with Mary McKinnon.

As he entered the room, he caught Mary's eye and she came rushing over, her arms outstretched in welcome. She was certainly a bonny lass with her curls and fair complexion and Alexander could see why his brother was attracted to her.

"Sit yourself down and I will pour you a cold ale, then you can tell me of your wedding plans." She rushed off and soon returned with a large handle of foaming beer and a glass of cider. "I'm so excited about the day but Hugh seems reluctant to say where we will live after the wedding."

Alexander was puzzled. Surely Hugh had told her of his plans to emigrate to New Zealand. "I guess he's busy tending to the stock. He's probably leaving the arrangements up to you."

"That must be it. I've already organized a larger room for us to share here at the inn, but I know that Hugh will often need to be away up in his hut on the hillside." Mary took a sip of her cider and smiled at him. "Tell me about your wedding arrangements. Hugh and I will be there for sure but will return to Salen after the celebrations."

They spent the next few minutes discussing his plans, but Alexander didn't mention that they were sailing soon afterwards. He would have to let his parents know before he discussed it with anyone else.

He caught the mail cart around the coast to Tobermory and was surprised at the number of travellers on the road all heading for town to enjoy the big event. Tobermory Bay was filled with small craft ready for the sailing and rowing competitions which would begin later in the day.

When he arrived at the Argyll Terrace cottages, there was no sign of life at his parents' house, so he went next door to where Christy was preparing a meal. She turned around in surprise and threw her arms around him.

"Our mother is at the school working with the children and old Archibald is down at the jetty helping with the boat racing. I believe my Donald is out in the back house working on some orders."

Alexander took a moment to congratulate his sister on her pregnancy, then walked along the path to talk with the child's father.

"Chirsty appears to be well," he said, as he took Donald's hand. "I am looking forward to the time when I have sons of my own."

"It's lucky that we were able to find this bonny cottage. With another child to consider we would have been really struggling back on Ulva," Donald admitted. "How are things looking back there?"

"Francis Clark is a fine farmer and the stock are healthy. Even though he was forced to clear the people from the island, he is basically a good man. As you know he has paid my passage to New Zealand and I will always be grateful for that."

Donald put down the boot that he was working on and looked at Alexander. "So you and Sally are definitely leaving on the great ship. Does your family know of your intention? They haven't mentioned it to anyone."

"I think our mother suspects something, but I will tell them while I am here. I need to talk to the men at the shipping office while I'm in town so maybe I should head that way now and perhaps catch up with my father."

"I'm finishing up soon and then we are all heading down to the bay to watch the boat racing. We'll see you down there no doubt."

Alexander left his bag in Christy's cottage and headed for the town. He passed the school and heard the excited voices of the children, and was soon at the busy waterfront where he walked past tables laden with goods for sale. Crowds of people were strolling about, enjoying the festive atmosphere. He passed the big hall where the Ceilidh would take place that evening. Banners and streamers adorned the building and a programme had been attached to a board beside the door.

The scene was such a busy one compared with life back on Ulva and Alexander was filled with excitement at what his life would be like a few weeks from now. He knew that after several months on a crowded ship they would reach the town of Dunedin and stay in barracks for a short time until they could travel to their allotted land.

He soon reached the offices of the shipping company and stood in line waiting for the clerk behind the desk to attend to him. He was surprised to see that there was a long line of men hopeful for a favourable response to their request to emigrate.

When he reached the desk and gave his name, the clerk reached up on to a high shelf and took down a pile of documents. He handed Alexander

128

a large brown package and asked for his signature.

"I think you will find all the necessary documents inside," he said. "You and your wife will need to be here to embark on the date set down, at least three hours before sailing time. You will need to bring everything that is on the list. Good luck to you sir."

Alexander took the package and walked out into the sunlight. He felt as if he was holding his whole future in his hands. Was he doing the right thing, leaving behind everything that was familiar?

He took a deep breath and clutching the package, walked along the waterfront and out onto the pier to try and locate his father. Sure enough, old Archibald was seated on a bench at the end of the pier. He had offered to help with the judging of the yacht races and held a sheet of paper attached to a board. The names of the yachts were listed on the paper and he was concentrating hard to read the words.

Archibald realized with a shock how much his father had aged since he had last seen him. His hair was thinning and his beard almost white. However, his eyes lit up when he noticed Alexander standing beside him.

"Welcome my son. This is quite a surprise. We were happy to meet your young lass a short time ago. The women were in quite a state of

129

excitement as they talked of your wedding plans."

Alexander smiled as he patted his father on the shoulder. Old Archibald was just the same, kindly man he had always been. He ran his eye over the list of names on the paper. Would his father be able to read the words? It wouldn't do any harm to stay for a while and help him out.

The first line of yachts was already at the start and when the gun was fired they set off, tacking into a stiff breeze. It was difficult to read the names on the craft or the numbers on their sails, but a young lad with a telescope was stationed beside them, reading out the names as the passed each mark.

As they crossed the finish line the names were read out and Alexander helped his father find them on the list and write their placing beside them. "I'm pleased to have your help. My eyes are not as good as they once were," his father smiled.

As the race finished, Archibald was able to hand the papers over to another official who was happy to take on the task. "Now we can go back and find the rest of the family," Archibald said, and together they walked back along the pier, keeping a look out for Margaret and the children.

In the mean time, old Margaret had returned home and Chirsty told her of Alexander's visit. "The children are all going down to the town together so we will meet them there," Margaret said. Chirsty called out to her husband to let him know that they were ready and soon they were off down the hill, anxious to be part of the activities in the town.

# Chapter 21

While the children from the other side of the island were preparing for their concert, Sarah Maclougas' father Neil was regretting his decision not to accompany his daughters on the journey to Tobermory.

"I feel that we are letting our daughter down, especially as she is to sing alone in that great hall."

Catherine gave a sigh. "The only reason for me to stay back was to take care of our baby, but if you want to go along then get yourself on a boat and out of here." She gave him a playful shove and smiled.

"Are you sure you don't mind if I go along? It would surely be a real treat to hear our daughter sing in the fine hall with her grandparents and so many of her aunts and cousins along to encourage her."

"Be off with you. I will cope until you return." Catherine smiled as Neil packed a small bag of clothing and set off to the jetty to take whatever craft was available for the journey to Tobermory.

He no sooner arrived at the pier than a fishing boat was about to cast off. It only took a wave of the hand and a few words before Neil was able to leap on board and settle in for the short trip around the coast.

The sight of Tobermory with all the sailing craft and small boats in the harbour was an exciting spectacle. Every inch of the bay was alive with vessels, large and small. It took a degree of skill for the boat master to bring his small craft up to the jetty where Neil was able to jump up onto the pier.

The first people he saw on landing were old Archibald and Alexander who were just heading back to meet the rest of the family gathered on the shore watching the action taking place on the water.

"Neil my friend. It is truly good to see you." Alexander grabbed his brother-in-law by the hand and soon they were surrounded by Chirsty and the children, with old Margaret keeping everyone in her sight.

Neil was so pleased to see his daughters enjoying the atmosphere and excitement of Tobermory, and the ecstatic look on young Sarah's face was ample reward for his sudden decision to make the journey. Once again he felt a desire to be part of the exciting world outside his small hillside community.

*********************

When Hugh McDonald returned to the inn after a day on the hillside, he was surprised to learn that his brother had been there that day. Mary was full of chatter about the wedding plans and how happy Alexander was to know that they would be travelling to Ulva for his marriage to Sally.

"They don't sound nearly as organized as we are. I'm not even sure where everyone will stay on Ulva. I believe Mr Clark is making some space available at the Mansion House and the ferry inn will no doubt be crowded."

"I thought we had planned to return here after the ceremony. After all, it will be our second night together." Hugh hugged Mary tightly, but as usual she pulled away.

"There will be enough time for that once we are wed. In the mean time there is so much to organize."

Hugh sipped his ale and looked around him. He found it difficult to envisage taking Mary away from this life where she was so comfortable and content. What did New Zealand have to offer a bright young woman?

He still hadn't made the bookings on the great ship and was loathe to broach the subject with his betrothed who was so immersed in their wedding plans. Perhaps he should let Alexander and Sally settle in New Zealand first and then follow later once they were established.

In the meantime, he sat and enjoyed the meal of beef and potatoes which was placed in front of him and relished in the warmth of the fire in the grate. There was certainly a lot to be said for the comfort of Salen town.

After an hour down on the waterfront, Chirsty was ready to return to her home and rest. The children should be resting too to prepare for the big night ahead of them.

Old Margaret was surprised to see her son-in-law Neil coming from the jetty and welcomed him. "You must stay in our cottage tonight and enjoy your daughter's singing. She was in fine voice at the rehearsal this afternoon. Everyone says she will be the star of the Ceilidh."

"I hope the occasion is not too much for her. Though I know she has had two excellent teachers for which I am grateful." Neil was feeling anxious at the huge responsiblity ahead for his young daughter. He knew she possessed a rare talent but had lived a very sheltered life in a remote area.

"I would like her to have every opportunity to further her talent which I feel is God given. But it is impossible for her to go any further on our small island." Neil had great ambitions for his daughter.

Before returning to Archibald and Margaret's home he decided to spend more time on the busy waterfront. A line of people outside an office near the pier caught his attention. He was surprised to learn that there were still vacancies on the ship which would take so many people across the vast seas to New Zealand where the opportunity to own land was so tempting.

It would do no harm to pick up some information and take it back to show his wife who was able to read and understand the English language far better than he was. Yes, Catherine would be able to explain the complicated documents on his return.

He stuffed a handful of papers into his bag and walked up the hill to Argyll Terrace where old Archibald was sitting on a bench looking out over the bay. They sat in silence for a while watching the boats sailing out in the harbour. The sun shone and a light breeze rippled through the flowering bushes.

"You have certainly found yourself a bonny home. I'm sure you have few regrets about making the move from Ulva." Archibald was quiet for a moment. "I vowed I would never leave the island and my heart remains there, but this place is certainly more comfortable for my wife and family." Archibald gave a sigh and lapsed into silence.

Just then old Margaret came bustling into view. The children had been given food and drink and were now supposed to be resting ready for their performance later in the evening.

"The merchants have been most generous. There is plenty of food for everyone and I'm sure the children are enjoying their visit." Margaret was tired but triumphant at the success of the plan to host the visiting children. But the big challenge still lay ahead when they had to perform in front of a crowded hall.

Archibald and Neil were full of praise for Margaret's efforts. "Our children will never forget this experience and I'm sure they will do themselves proud," said Neil, as he gave his mother-in-law an encouraging pat on the shoulder. "Now you must rest so you can enjoy tonight's performances."

# Chapter 22

The biggest crowd for years was assembling in the town hall on Tobermory's waterfront. Most of the seats were already filled and the performers were waiting nervously in a room at the back, eyeing each other anxiously.

The children were smartly attired in their various colours with black and white or tartan outfits to the fore. Adult performers were also seated around the edge of the room clutching a programme which listed the order of performances.

Young Sarah Maclougas sat between her cousins, wearing a red sash over her black skirt and crisp white blouse. She nervously chewed a finger nail as she looked around for her teacher.

Angus McLean looked across and smiled. He waved his fiddle in the air and gave her an encouraging wink. "You'll be fine," he mouthed, although he was probably as nervous as his pupils. Luckily their turn would come soon and they could relax and enjoy the rest of the Ceilidh.

A round of applause sounded as the first group entered the hall. They were to perform a Scottish folk dance and soon the floor was shaking as they swung into their rhythm. The audience was clapping along in time to the beat, including the McDonald and McArthur families who had been given seats close to the front of the hall.

A young woman sang a simple ballad next and then the first group of school children trooped out into the hall. Donald and Chirsty held their breath as young Margaret and Ketty scraped their way through a tune, their fiddles held tightly. The pianist kept the children together and everybody applauded loudly at the end of the item.

"That wasn't too bad," old Margaret smiled. "It actually sounded better than I imagined after hearing the practices."

A second group of Tobermory children were next to take the stage with their teacher Archie Campbell conducting them as they sang a selection of old songs, unaccompanied and in two part harmony.

The audience gave them a great round of applause and the children responded with a deep bow and joined their classmates at the back of the hall.

Neil Maclougas was getting more anxious as time went on. The items were of a very high standard and he was afraid that Archie McLean's pupils would sound inferior. But then they walked out onto the stage, their heads held high. Archie had his fiddle poised and led them into the first number. Their voices were clear and true and then came the moment the families had been waiting for.

Tears filled their eyes as young Sarah moved to the front of the stage and the first plaintiff notes of 'Windsong' filled the hall. The eerie wail of the strings echoed the sound of the sea and when the young girl began to sing there was a stunned silence. The clear rich tone took them to another place where the sounds of nature blended together.

The rest of the children joined in the final chorus and when the last notes faded away, the audience was on their feet, clapping and shouting their approval. Sarah blushed and stood awkwardly in the centre of the stage unsure how to react, until her teacher took her hand and held it in the air to acknowledge the applause.

Luckily it was time for the interval and a chance for everyone to move around and congratulate the children who had performed so well. Adult choirs and several dancers were to perform in the second half so the excited youngsters were given drinks and a snack and allowed to mix with the audience to enjoy the rest of the show.

Old Margaret gave her grand daughter a huge hug. "I am so proud of you. I'm proud of all of you." She looked around at all the shining faces. "I feel truly blessed to have such a family."

********************

Alexander and Sally were enjoying a rare day off together. With all the excitement of the Ceilidh, he had still not found the opportunity to tell his parents about his plans to leave on the great ship. He hadn't caught up with his brother either, but in the mean time Sally was packing a few precious belongings into the tin trunk which they would take to New Zealand. She hugged the warm blankets and linen table cloths as she packed them inside.

"I'm not sure where our bed will come from or what sort of table we will have." Alexander studied the contents of the chest. "But I'm sure we will find everything we need once we arrive in the new land."

"You have been promised employment and I'm sure there would be some sort of work for me." Sally continued folding the dresses and undergarments which she would be taking. Who knew where she would get her next set of clothing?

"I can't believe our wedding is only two weeks away. Do you know how many of your family are likely to attend?" Sally's own family all lived close by on Ulva or just across the narrow strip of water which separated Ulva from the larger island of Mull and would be returning home after the celebrations.

"We have arranged for my parents and Chirsty to stay at the Ulva Inn. Hugh and Mary will return to Salen but I'm not sure about the number of children."

"Never fear. We can set them up in the barn at Ulva House. There is plenty of soft hay and straw for them to sleep on." Sally was looking forward to their wedding day but was very relaxed about the details. Her thoughts were mainly on preparing for the long sea voyage ahead.

Alexander had been given a detailed list of all they would need for the journey. They knew that their accommodation would be cramped but they would need to be self sufficient when they arrived in their new land.

As the afternoon was warm, Alexander suggested a walk along the track to the top of the hill where they could look down over the remaining cottages dotted along the water's edge. Many had been destroyed as the tenants left and the few remaining were grim reminders of a once flourishing village where harvesting kelp had been the greatest source of income.

The breeze rustled the bushes as they clamboured up the hillside, following the sheep tracks and avoiding the clumps of heather that grew profusely among the rocks. Flocks of sheep gathered together as they approached and eagles soured overhead searching for a meal.

"I'm sure my father still misses the peace and quiet of Ulva but he appears to have settled well in Tobermory. I'm sure we too will think of this place with fondness when we are far away on foreign soil." Alexander looked around him and sighed. New Zealand seemed a very long way from Scotland.

"We will make the most of our opportunity and build ourselves a home to be proud of." Sally put her arms around Alexander's waist and held him tight. "Now come on. Let's visit the old church and see what needs to be done."

The church yard was looking tidier, the interior was now clean and the woodwork gleamed with polish. Once the floral arrangements were in place the building would be fit for the grandest of weddings.

******************

With the excitement of the Ceilidh behind them it was soon time for the visiting children to return to their homes. Most of the Tobermory children were at the jetty to see them off as many friendships had been forged in the few days they had been together. Margaret and the other women spent the afternoon sorting the bedding and furniture and chatted happily about the success of the visit.

"I feel there is a great future for your grand daughter Sarah," they enthused. "She surely has the voice of an angel."

Margaret knew that the young girl had a great talent, but there would be little opportunity to develop it in such a remote part of the island. "I hope she gets the chance to use her gift. She is lucky that her school teacher is musically inclined and will be able to train her to some extent."

Neil Maclougas was quiet on the way back around the coast. The papers he had collected from the shipping office were packed away in his bag but he wasn't looking forward to broaching the subject with his wife. He knew that Catherine would support him in whatever decision he made, but the thought of undertaking such a long journey with so many young children was an intimidating prospect.

His oldest daughter was still excited after her great success at the Ceilidh where she had been awarded a special prize for the most promising performance and young Angus McLean was bursting with pride at the talent shown by his pupils.

"That was a glorious moment, when the audience was silent and then burst into wild applause. I will treasure it for ever," he confided as the two men stood together leaning against the boat's rail.

"Yes, you are right. Old Archie Campbell taught the children well and you are continuing to maintain the high standard. I'm sure much good will come from this experience."

It was almost an hour before the small craft reached the jetty where the children were to disembark. Although it was Sunday most of the villagers had gathered to welcome the young people and to hear all their news.

There was a loud cheer from the crowd as the boat was tied to the pier and the boatman began to unload the luggage and boxes as the children scrambled ashore. Catherine was one of the first to gather her children in her arms. The new baby was wrapped in a shawl and she laughed and put out her arms when she saw her sisters.

"She has missed you. See how pleased she is to see you return safely." Catherine turned to Neil and handed him the infant as she helped sort the girls' belongings. Sarah was bursting to tell her mother about receiving the top prize but Angus McLean was first to share the news.

"Our children were the stars of the show and your daughter was unbelievable. We were so proud of her." He shook Catherine by the hand before he picked up his bundle and the precious fiddle and shepherded the remaining children up the hill away from the jetty.

There were happy scenes in the Maclougas household that night as Neil and his daughters described the events of the past few days. They admired the silver cup which Margaret had received and placed it on a shelf above the smoky fireplace.

"We are so fortunate to have such talented children," Neil said. "I feel we should try to give them every opportunity to succeed in life."

145

Catherine sensed that her husband was discontented, but said little. Whatever was on his mind could wait another day. Tonight was a time for celebration.

# Chapter 23

Now that Hugh McDonald had abandoned the idea of leaving on the great ship for New Zealand he decided to make the best of things and show some enthusiasm for the wedding plans. The idea of living at the crowded inn held little appeal so he started to look around for a suitable dwelling for himself and his new bride.

His uncle John MacDonald had been one of the first to occupy the cottages built by Lachlan McQuarrie in the village of Salen and after making a few enquiries, Hugh discovered that the small dwelling would soon be vacant as his cousin Charles and his wife were moving onto a property on the main land.

He felt cheerful as he dined with Mary at the inn that night. "Mary, my love, I think I have found us the perfect place to live."

Mary smiled hesitantly, unsure of what he was about to suggest. She hoped he had forgotten his idea about leaving Scotland and taking the great ship to the other side of the world. "What have you got in mind, my dear? I don't need to live in a fine house as long as we are together."

"Come with me and take a look." Hugh took Mary on to the paved street and walked past the jetty and along the line of McQuarrie cottages. "What do you say about living here with me?" She gasped. Never in her greatest expectations had she imagined living in a place such as this.

"Are you sure we can do this? It is the grandest of cottages. I would be most happy to live here." She hugged Hugh and danced around, unable to contain her excitement. "I was sure you were still intent on travelling to the other side of the world. I will be very happy to stay here in Salen."

"My brother Alexander is set to travel across the sea and perhaps we will follow him some day, but in the meantime, this will be our home." Hugh took Mary into his arms and this time she didn't resist. They kissed long and hard and when he returned her to the inn she took him by the hand and led him into her room.

"I am so happy and we will be wed in two weeks' time. Lie with me for a while and teach me what I need to know." Hugh hesitated for a moment. Mary had always been so much against any intimacy until their wedding day. Surely she was not about to change her mind?

He took her in his arms as they lay on the narrow cot. She had kicked off her boots and he could imagine her bare legs around him. He pulled off his jacket as she removed her coat. As they lay together he felt the warmth of her body against him. Her breasts were firm as he held her against his chest.

Their kisses were long and lingering but when his hand began to reach under her shift, Mary pushed his arm away. "I'm sorry. I can't do this until after we are wed."

148

Hugh lifted his body and moved away. They lay still for several minutes until he reluctantly stood and straightened his clothing. "I've waited this long. I guess I can be patient a little longer."

Mary curled up on the bed, her face red with embarrassment. The walls were thin and her room mate might appear at any time. She wanted their first time together to be special.

"I do love you Hugh, but this is not the right time and place to offer you my body. I promise that I will be truly yours on our wedding night."

"I do understand, my dear, but now I will leave before I am tempted to make you change your mind." Hugh leant over and gave Mary a hasty kiss, then picked up his jacket and left to spend another night alone in his small hut behind the barn. Tomorrow he would meet Charles and make arrangements to rent the Salen cottage.

********************

With the bundle of papers still packed in his bag, Neil Maclougas knew he could waste no time before sharing the information with his wife. Catherine's eyes opened wide when she saw the documents in his hand. She sat down abruptly and began to read the words on the pages.

Free passages were being offered on the vessel with 10 pounds to be paid back at a later date.

Twenty acres of land was being granted to each married couple and each child was also being granted a small piece of land.

"This would certainly be a great opportunity for our children. I've heard that conditions in the new city are very favourable." Neil broke the silence. "The only problem I see is the length of the journey as we would be on the boat for several months."

Catherine was fearful but felt a tinge of excitement at the prospect. She knew that Alexander and Sally would be with them and could share the burden of looking after the children.

"But the ship leaves in one month. Surely we couldn't have everything ready in such a short time."

"If you agree, I will return to Tobermory tomorrow and register our interest. I'm not even sure whether we would be accepted. Then I will purchase a number of cabin trunks to pack our belongings."

Catherine could see that her husband was excited at the prospect of sailing to New Zealand. It had obviously been on his mind for some time and she thought that she would cope with the help of her brother and his new wife.

She looked around at the small crowded dwelling with its mud floor and smoky interior and knew that there must be a better way to live.

Although she would miss her parents and the rest of the family, she would find many Scottish families to befriend in the new land.

*********************

Since moving to Tobermory, Donald Macarthur had built up a reputation as a cobbler and received many requests to repair shoes and boots. When time allowed he also enjoyed turning the best leather into fashionable shoes and slippers which were mostly sold across the water in the larger town of Oban. A new stock of leather had just arrived and the small back house behind the main dwelling was full to overflowing. There was no way he could have managed in the small croft back on Ulva with all the children underfoot.

Chirsty came out to join him. "Business seems to be good. Perhaps it is time you visited the stores in Oban to check out the latest styles. I think the ladies of the town would appreciate your shoemaking skills."

Donald took her in his arms. "Maybe you should come with me. We could take the ferry and spend the day over on the main land."

"I would have to find a dress that fits, but it would be a chance to choose wedding gifts for my brothers." Chirsty was excited at the thought of spending a day in the bustling town of Oban. She had done little but care for her family over the past few months and knew that her mother would be happy to look out for the children.

"Speaking of your brothers, have you heard any more about their plans to take the ship to New Zealand? Alexander mentioned it when he was here over the weekend but I haven't heard anything from young Hugh."

"I don't think my parents have been told of their plans. I know Alexander is almost certainly going on the ship but I don't think Hugh's bride is the least bit keen." Chirsty would miss her brothers but was glad that Donald was not talking about making the long journey across the sea.

They decided to visit Oban the following day, so Chirsty crossed the yard to her mother's house to seek her help. Donald and old Archibald had planted a garden which stretched across both properties and rows of colourful flowers and vegetables were flourishing in the sheltered plots.

Old Margaret was only too happy to get the children ready for school and take care of young Archibald during the day. She helped Chirsty select a suitable skirt and blouse to wear to the larger town as well as a newly woven shawl to wear around her shoulders. "You will enjoy a day away from the young ones and I know they will be no trouble."

Chirsty felt light hearted as she searched through her garments to find a tidy hat and bag. They would have to leave early on the mail cart to catch the ferry from Craignure but would have a whole day in Oban where they could visit the stores and perhaps enjoy a meal at the prestigious Craig-Ard Hotel.

The mist was just clearing from over the bay when Donald and Chirsty lined up to travel on the mail cart which would take them to the ferry. Chirsty climbed aboard the cart and sat down on the seat behind the driver while Donald helped load the mail and clamboured aboard.

Soon they were on their way, along the narrow road which straddled the coast line. There were a few stops on the way to pick up mail, but soon the Craignure jetty was in sight and the MacBrayne ferry ready to set off across the water to the grand town of Oban.

Once aboard, Chirsty settled in the cabin while her husband went to the very front of the vessel to view the sights. As the island slipped away the mainland came into view with its ancient castles and elegant villas and hotels along the shore.

Donald took Chirsty by the hand as they disembarked from the ferry. They walked along the cobbled street towards the major stores and boarding houses. The town was alive with residents and visitors arriving by coach or steamer, many hoping to explore the ancient monastery on Iona or the mysterious underwater caves of Staffa.

But Donald knew where he was headed. There were three stores that carried his footwear and he intended to call on them and check out his competition. Chirsty was taken aback at the shops with their plate glass windows and the variety of goods on display. She pulled her shawl a little closer around her shoulders as she eyed the clothing and linen goods laid out on racks and shelves.

Perhaps a linen sheet or pillow case as a wedding gift and she would dearly love to take something back for her parents to brighten their humble home. With Donald's help, she chose a linen tablecloth for each of her brothers and a metal serving spoon for her mother. Some bright ribbons for her daughters' hair were also included in the parcel.

With the profits from the sale of his footwear in his pocket, Donald was able to buy them a meal at the new hotel, though Chirsty felt somewhat shabby alongside the well dressed tourists.

Roast pork and vegetables, followed by a delicious apple pie with cream was a welcome change from the simple diet they were used to and Chirsty felt as though she had entered a new world. "We will have to bring the children here to see this marvelous place," she said, as they walked back towards the wharf where the ferry was waiting.

"I have ordered some new patterns for slippers and buttoned boots and hopefully if these prove popular we will be able to make this journey more often." Donald was confident that his business was beginning to prosper. It was good to see Chirsty in such high spirits and he knew his children would love to visit this vibrant town.

*********************

Back in Tobermory Margaret was busy keeping her eye on young Archibald who was full of curiosity and inclined to wander. Her husband was away on the lobster boat and would not be back until nightfall, so she set off with her grandson into the town which was still buzzing from the excitement of the successful Ceilidh.

The visiting children had created such an interest that the people were determined that they should be invited back next year. "It was hard to believe that there was so much talent coming from such a remote part of Mull." The butcher who had supplied the meat for the visitors was impressed. "Perhaps the invitation needs to go out to other communities around the island."

Margaret agreed that the occasion had been a huge success but she was feeling weary from all the work it had involved. "I would leave it to the younger women to arrange it next year."

As she walked past the end of the jetty she was surprised to see her son-in-law Neil Maclougas coming into view. "What are you doing back in these parts? We don't usually see too much of you here in Tobermory.

Neil looked embarrassed. He didn't want to let old Margaret know of their plans until they were finalised. He had left the application at the shipping office but had to wait for their journey to be confirmed.

"We may be looking at moving to another place where the children could benefit. I would like to see young Sarah have a chance to further her talent."

"I agree that she needs to be encouraged. Everyone is still talking about her fine voice. Perhaps you should look at moving to Oban. Donald and Chirsty are there right now and I believe it is a town full of opportunity."

"You may be right. But I must return home tonight so I will be on my way." Neil walked back along the pier to catch a ride in a fishing boat around to his part of the island. He didn't want to say too much to old Margaret until he was certain of their plans.

Margaret allowed little Archibald to spend some time playing in the soft sand alongside the jetty. He was soon busy arranging a row of sticks and shells and was reluctant to leave the game and return to the Argyll Terrace cottage.

"Come along Archibald. The children will be home from school soon and ready for something to eat." Brushing the sand from his knees, he did what she asked, and soon they were making their way back up the steep hill towards the church and school.

Margaret was a little puzzled at her meeting with Neil Maclougas. It was very unusual for the hard-working shepherd to venture into the town and to see him there two days in a row was something of a mystery.

By the time she had walked back up the steep slope the children were spilling out of the school gates. Their teacher Archie Campbell was standing by the side of the road to see the little ones safely on their way. "Good afternoon Mrs McDonald. Thank you again for all your help with the visiting children. They really proved to be most popular at the Ceilidh."

"I agree, Mr Campbell, but it was mostly your early teaching which produced such a high standard. I'm happy that the young school master is following in your footsteps."

"That is very true. But your young grand daughter has a talent that needs to be addressed. The time will come when she will need a teacher who can help her reach her full potential." Archie Campbell was concerned that such a gift would not be developed in such a remote part of the island.

"I'm sure her parents are well aware of the situation and will find a way to solve the problem. But now I must get these children home and prepare a meal before their parents return from Oban."

Margaret gathered the children together and herded them across the road. They ran ahead and crowded into the small room where she kept her spinning wheel and weaving loom. The girls were always fascinated at the patterns produced on the loom and begged their grand mother to show them how it was done.

Time passed quickly and they were all fed and ready for bed long before Donald and Chirsty returned on the cart from Craignure, after a busy and exciting day.

# Chapter 24

With two sons about to be married a day apart, Margaret and Archibald knew they would be staying for two nights at the Ulva Inn. It had been many years since the inn was managed by Alexander Shaw who was married to Margaret's younger sister Bell Curry.  The family had joined the exodus to Canada back in the 1840s and flourished in the province of Ontario. It would be strange to be staying at the inn after so many years but Margaret knew they would be comfortable there and transport had been arranged from  Salen following Hugh and Mary's wedding at the handsome stone church.

Archibald was especially looking forward to being back on Ulva and attending church on the island for the wedding of Alexander and Sally. Margaret had been busy weaving cosy blankets as a wedding gift and they were also supplying some of the drinks which would follow the two ceremonies.

"It would have been easier to arrange a double wedding at Salen and just one wedding feast, but I guess the women each want their own special day," said Chirsty as she tried to work out how she and Donald would get all the children over to the island. She and her parents were to stay at the inn and Donald would look after the rest of the family at Ulva Mansion House where bedding had been arranged in one of the large barns on the property.

"You are right, but it is such an exciting time for both of them. I know Alexander and Hugh will have all the arrangements under control." Margaret was most happy with her new church in Tobermory but was looking forward to being back in the two churches where so many family events had been celebrated. There had been happy occasions and many sad ones as well, especially the funerals of her sister Ann and both her parents who were all buried at Pennygown.

Several of her children had been baptised at the smaller church on Ulva, but only when a minister could be persuaded to make the journey from Mull. She hoped that all their children would be able to attend the weddings but she hadn't heard back from her two older daughters, Mary and Sarah, or sons, Donald and John, who were all living on different parts of the main land, some as far away as Ayrshire.

✱✱✱✱✱✱✱✱✱✱✱✱✱✱✱✱✱✱

When the big day came for the wedding of Hugh and Mary, the families were up early ready to make the journey along the road to Salen. Margaret and Archibald were seated up the front with the driver while Donald and Chirsty and all the young ones crowded on the back of the wagon.

Everyone was in high spirits as they were jolted over the bumpy road. Donald and Chirsty pointed out the sights as they drove along the Sound of Mull, past small settlements and ancient stones until the Craignure ferry buildings came into view.

Here they stopped for a time to stretch their legs and use the privy, before turning on to the road which would take them to Salen. Margaret pointed out the grave stones as they passed by Pennygown and explained to the children that their great grand father was buried there.

"Can we stop and have a look?" Young John was fascinated by the head stones, but his mother shook her head. There would be no time to linger today.

Back at the inn, Mary was in such a state of nervousness that her bridesmaid, Annie, suggested a brisk walk around the village to calm her down. "You have looked forward to this day for so long, you must relax and enjoy every moment of it," she admonished her friend.

All the preparations had been carried out the day before and the church was polished and ready for the ceremony. Tall containers of flowers had been placed around the walls and a large garland was ready for Mary to carry into the church.

Her dress and head gear were laid out on the bed along with the fine linen undergarments.

The inn keeper had made sure that all the food was prepared and ready to be heated later. The ceremony was planned for late morning and then the feasting would begin around noon. This would allow plenty of time for the families to make the short journey over to Ulva where they would stay the night in readiness for the second ceremony the next day.

While Mary was trying to calm her nerves at the Salen inn, Hugh was pacing around his small room back at the farm. His friends were amused at his agitation "Never fear, Hugh my lad. Your pretty bride will be waiting for you in the church." His older friend was full of advice.

"Make the most of your last moments of freedom. You will soon have a wife to answer to," laughed another.

But soon it was time for Hugh to walk the two miles into Salen. His good jacket and trousers were already at the inn where he would change on his arrival. He and Mary would be moving into the Salen cottage in a week's time and in the meantime they could share a room at the inn.

Hugh had mixed feelings as he strode along the dusty track. He knew he wanted to marry his beloved Mary, but he wasn't sure that living in the village of Salen was the right choice. His heart was still set on making the move to the new country of New Zealand.

*******************

As the cart clattered over the cobblestones through the village, Margaret McDonald caught sight of her son as he headed for the inn. "Hugh, my love. How are you feeling on such an important day?"

Hugh was caught by surprise to see so many of his family crowded onto the cart.

"I'm not sure how I feel right now. But I'm sure I will be relieved when all the fuss is behind us.'

Donald laughed. "I felt the same way when Chirsty and I were about to be wed. It's a big step you are taking for sure, but well worth it, I can tell you."

Hugh helped his mother and children down from the cart and then took his leave as he needed to wash and change before heading to the church.

The cart was soon unpacked and all their gear stowed away at the inn where they were offered refreshments and a chance to tidy themselves ready for the ceremony. There was no sign of young Mary who was probably feeling just as nervous as Hugh appeared to be.

Ketty and Margaret dusted their boots and tied the new ribbons in their hair. "Can we go and see the bride?" they asked. "No, my dears. You must wait until she walks into the church. Then everyone will be able to admire her." Chirsty

163

smiled at the excitement this wedding was creating.

The two little boys were more interested in looking around the inn and peeping into the kitchen where the food smelt so appetising.

At that moment, Alexander and Sally appeared at the door and there were more shrieks of excitement. To make the day even more memorable, friends and family members began to congregate in the large room. Margaret was delighted to see her daughters who had made the journey from Oban that morning.

"I'm not sure where we will stay, but we are here for both weddings," said the eldest. "I'm sure someone will find a bed for us overnight."

Alexander was overjoyed to see his sisters and introduced them to his bride to be. The women hugged Sally and welcomed her into the family.

"Now I think it is time we made our way to the church.  We will want to get good seats near the front." Margaret soon had everyone organized and the happy group made their way across the road, laughing and talking as they went.

They were surprised to find the building more than half filled already. Mary's family had already taken up the front pew on one side and the other had been left for Archibald and Margaret. Chirsty and the two girls also squeezed into the narrow seat and for a moment they all bowed their heads in silent prayer.

Margaret looked around and was surprised that so many of their old friends were here to witness the wedding. She was sorry that Catherine and Neil had not been able to attend. Neil was busy with lambing and Catherine was not eager to make the journey alone with the children.

People spoke in hushed whispers especially when Hugh and Alexander made their way to the front of the church waiting for the bride to appear. Then there was a rumble of music from the organ and everyone stood and looked around.

Mary stood framed in the doorway and there was a gasp as she looked so beautiful. The gown and head dress, along with the floral bouquet, were perfect and Hugh could hardly take his eyes off her as she made her way up the narrow aisle, clutching her father's arm.

Her bridesmaid Annie also looked delightful as she adjusted Mary's veil and took the flowers from her ready for the ceremony to begin.

Rev Campbell's deep voice rumbled on, the familiar words of the wedding ceremony reverberating around the church. Sally hugged herself and looked towards Alexander who stood near the altar, handsome in his borrowed suit. Tomorrow they would be wed and she could hardly wait.

All too soon, the bridal march was being played and the bride and groom led the wedding party from the church. The crowd shuffled out and threw flower petals over the couple, the church grounds soon turning into a sea of colour.

Mary looked up at Hugh and they exchanged a quick kiss, before setting off across the road to the inn to enjoy the festivities. Drinks were poured and a toast was offered to the new couple before the meal was served.

# Chapter 25

It was late afternoon before Margaret and Archibald left the inn and were driven across the island, past Gruline to the Ulva Ferry landing. "That was such a pretty wedding. Hugh and Mary looked so happy." Margaret sighed as she settled onto the hard wooden seat.

"Indeed it was a great occasion, my dear. But now I am looking forward to setting foot back on the Ulva." Archibald was tired, but eager to catch the first glimpse of his beloved island.

The two older girls had remained at the Salen Inn but the rest of the family were following in hired carts. The small boat made two trips across the narrow strip of water to ferry everybody onto the island. Luckily the inn was close to the ferry landing and Ulva House only a short walk away.

The boat man was pleased to welcome the family and Archibald was overjoyed to be back on the familiar jetty. Black crows and sea birds gave him a noisy welcome and he stood for a moment, breathing in the salty air, as the bags were unloaded.

Chirsty and Donald arrived on the second boat. The children were whirling around with excitement and raced up to the door of the building where the inn keeper was waiting.

"Come on, you rascals. We have a little further to go." Donald steered the children up the track to

Ulva House where their accommodation was waiting.

"We will get settled in and come back and join you," he said as he left an exhausted Chirsty with her parents. "We will all dine at the inn tonight."

The interior of the inn was dark as they stepped in from the sunlight, but they were led into a cheery room overlooking the jetty. A boy carried their bags to their allotted rooms while a maid brought them a tray with tea and biscuits and set it on the polished table.

"You are to rest and enjoy our hospitality," she said as she poured the tea into patterned cups. Margaret was thoroughly enjoying being fussed over while Archibald looked around with interest. The inn had been refurbished since he last visited as it was an excellent stop off for visitors to the attractions of Staffa and the wonder of the basalt columns of Fingal's Cave.

Chirsty took the opportunity to lie on the bed and rest. She knew that Sally and Alexander would help Donald set up the beds for the children back at the barn behind Ulva House.

Alexander and Sally were pleased with the distraction as they showed Donald and the children where they would be sleeping. Sally was nervous about her big day ahead, especially as Hugh and Mary's wedding had been so perfect.

"We will feed the children tonight while you go to the inn and catch up with Chirsty and your parents," Alexander instructed.

As the children explored the farm buildings and little Archibald chased the turkeys, Donald was pleased to take the track back to the inn where Chirsty was waiting. He would return later and sleep with the young ones, but for the moment he would enjoy the hospitality at the inn.

***********************

The next day dawned bright and sunny, with no sign of the wind that often blew on Ulva. Archibald was up early and walked along the shore towards Ardalum from where glimpses of Ardglass and Soriby could be obtained. He climbed the hill and looked down on the abandoned villages where he had lived and worked for so many years.

The sight was a depressing one and he turned and made his way back to the cheerful company at the inn. There was no life for him back on Ulva, that was for sure. The first boat had just pulled into the ferry landing with Hugh and Mary, along with his daughters, Mary and Sarah, among its passengers. It had been many months since so many of his family members had gathered in one place and he felt at peace.

169

Several of Sally's family were also alighting from the boat and were soon gathering outside the inn while two of Sally's brothers and their wives came into view, having walked along the trail from Ormaig.

The inn keeper beckoned them inside and offered refreshments and the women took the opportunity to tidy their hair and smooth their clothing before heading along the track which led to the church. The minister had arrived and the service was due to start in about an hour so the crowd gradually moved in the direction of the church.

Chirsty kept an anxious eye out for Donald and the children. "I do hope they are clean and tidy," she said, "Perhaps I should have gone over to Ulva House to supervise them."

"I know that Donald and the older girls will manage," Margaret assured her. "I'm sure they will be here in time for the ceremony."

By now, a large crowd had gathered in the grounds of the church and Chirsty could hear the music as they approached the building. She was surprised that Donald and the children were already there, faces scrubbed and hair neatly plaited.

And now Alexander and Hugh came striding along the track and it was time to go inside and wait for the ceremony to begin. There was a great deal of chatter as the people waited for the bride to appear. On a signal from the minister, they stood and turned towards the door.

Sally looked very tall and elegant in her long dress and train. She held her father's arm and beamed as she saw Alexander standing at the front of the church. She practically dragged her father up the aisle, then stood beside Alexander, her face pink with embarrassment. There was a muffled laugh from the congregation as Alexander gave her arm a squeeze, then stood facing the minister.

Rev Campbell repeated the same words as yesterday, but they sounded louder in the small church. Then it was time for Alexander to put a ring on her finger and they clung to each other until the minister instructed them to move back through the church.

There was lots of merriment as the crowd surged from the church and stood around outside. People were hugging Sally and clapping Alexander on the back. The children ran about throwing bunches of flowers and petals over everyone who got in the way.

"This wedding is much more fun than yesterday," observed Chirsty. "I think Alexander has found himself a spirited wife."

"Both weddings were beautiful and a credit to the young couples." Margaret didn't want to make any comparisons. Hugh and Mary sat near the back of the church during the ceremony. They had spent their first night together at the inn but still had not consummated their marriage. Mary had undressed down to her fine undergarments and Hugh had undressed completely, but the events of the day had caught up with them and dimmed their desire.

Mary felt guilty as she glanced across at her husband. Maybe tonight when they returned to their room at the Salen inn she would relax and they would really become man and wife.

But now it was time to make their way to Ulva House where a feast awaited and music would be enjoyed. The crowd followed the old pathway until they were in sight of the farm buildings. The children rushed ahead while the adults followed more sedately.

The celebrations were about to begin. Alexander took Sally by the hand and led her along the track. He was so proud of his beautiful bride and knew that once the crowd left, they would make love into the night. She leant over and kissed him passionately. This was the start of a whole new life.

The sound of bagpipes set the scene as Alexander and Sally walked through the gates of Ulva House where a shelter had been set up on the lawn and food and drinks laid out on long tables. A tartan clad piper was stationed in the corner of the yard and Lamont and McDonald tartan ribbons swung gaily in the breeze.

The crowd stood in wonder at the colourful display then made their way to the tables to fill their glasses and partake of the food. Francis Clark had been most generous in supplying meat and poultry and Sally's family and friends on the island had all contributed to the feast.

The festivities went long into the night. The first to leave were Hugh and Mary, along with Alexander's older sisters who were all returning to the inn at Salen. Even Archibald and Margaret stayed up till after midnight and the children drifted off to their beds in the barn a little later.

There was much good natured laughter as Alexander finally took Sally off to the room they were sharing. They were bombarded with flowers and the fiddles played a merry tune as the happy couple disappeared to spend their first night together.

# Chapter 26

Back on the far side of Mull, Catherine regretted not attending her brothers' weddings. "If we go on the ship to New Zealand I might not see many of my family again," she lamented.

"I'm sure it is God's will that we take this opportunity to improve the lives of our children, and Alexander and Sally will be with us." Neil did his best to calm his wife down. This was not the time to have second thoughts.

As she busied herself around the crowded hovel in which they lived, Catherine tried to look on the positive side. She knew that Neil would never be satisfied remaining on Mull and the chance to farm their own land was an exciting one. Several of their acquaintances had already left the island for other parts of the world so they would not be alone once they landed on the shores of New Zealand.

"You are right. I'm not looking forward to the long sea voyage but we will be in good company."

It was time for Neil to leave for the hills and the lambing beat. He would sleep in a small hut on the hill top tonight so he clutched a bag of food and warm clothing and set off up the steep track. With any luck, this time next year he would have his own flock of sheep and be his own master.

Catherine sent the girls to gather mussels along the shoreline while the boys were told to fetch some wood to keep the fire burning. Then she sat in the sun, nursing little Mary Ann and contemplating their future.

***********************

With the excitement of the wedding celebrations behind them, it was time for Margaret and Archibald to make their way back to Tobermory. Just as they were leaving the Ulva inn, Alexander and Sally came into view, followed by Donald and the McArthur children.

"These two days have been the happiest time and I fear that life will be very dull for a while." Margaret gave Sally a hug. She was delighted with her new daughter-in-law and looked forward to getting to know her better.

Alexander looked solemn as he stood before his parents. He was about to give them some disturbing news. "I didn't want to spoil things for you, but I really can't wait any longer to tell you of our plans."

Margaret's heart sunk and Archibald's face grew pale as they listened to what Alexander had to say. Although they had heard whispers about their son's plans to emigrate, they had not wanted to believe them.

"Sally and I are to leave for New Zealand in two weeks' time on the great ship. It is such a fine opportunity and Francis Clark is lending us his support.”

“Oh my dears, I know it is a chance for you to better yourselves. But we will miss you greatly. It is as though the strands that hold the family together are to be torn apart.”

“We will write to you with every detail of our new life. We will never allow the strands to be broken.” Sally spoke quietly, but with conviction. “There are many of our villagers travelling on the ship and we will establish our own community, of that I am sure.”

Margaret thought back to the time when her Curry family set off for Canada. She had felt the same way back then, but life went on and they received news of the family once in a while.

“Is your brother Hugh leaving as well? He has seemed a little reluctant to talk of his plans.”

“I know he is keen to make the journey but I fear that his new bride has persuaded him to change his mind.” Alexander felt sad that his brother was not accompanying them to New Zealand. He knew that Hugh had been excited at the prospect.

Archibald pulled himself together and shook his son’s hand. “We can’t begrudge you the opportunity. When I was a younger man I might have been tempted to join you. You go with our blessing.”

Alexander turned away so his father could not see the tears forming in his eyes. These next two weeks were going to be very difficult indeed. Sally took his hand in support. She had already told her family of their plans but had warned them not to spread the news until Archibald and Margaret had been told.

The news came as no surprise to Donald and Chirsty as they had suspected all along that Alexander and Hugh were planning to leave on the ship. "I think Hugh will be disappointed. He had his heart set on going, but his new bride has apparently had her way." Chirsty was disappointed for her brother and hoped that his wife would support and encourage him in the future.

By now the small boat had carried them back to the jetty on Mull where a farm cart was waiting to take them to Salen. They had planned to meet up with Hugh and Mary before making the homeward journey.

Mary and Hugh had news of their own when they arrived, telling them that they were to live in the cottage once tenanted by Margaret's sister Ann and her family. "That is great news. I was afraid that you were planning on leaving for New Zealand with your brother." Margaret was very impressed. The Salen cottage had been a fine home for John MacDonald and her sister and held many memories, both happy and sad. After Ann's death, John had remarried and added to his family, but a few years later he was widowed once more.

Mary talked happily about the weddings and plans for the new cottage. "Hugh is taking me to Oban in the morning where we will spend a few days until our new home is ready," she said.

Margaret smiled at her enthusiasm and hoped that her younger son would get over his disappointment soon. "I'm sure you will be very content and make the most of your chances," was her final comment.

**********************

After the trip to Ulva, Margaret noticed that Archibald was tiring more readily. At times he appeared to be out of breath and she thought it might be time to consult Dr MacColl who had looked after the family for so many years.

"I think that your husband is working too hard and should give up his job on the lobster boats," he said after giving old Archibald a thorough check. "He is not a young man any more and his heart has weakened."

Margaret was concerned and asked Chirsty to help her tell her father the news. "I'm not sure how we will manage without his income." Margaret was worried, but Chirsty assured her that they would help out, especially as the older girls practically lived with their grandparents.

Chirsty also knew that with a little encouragement, old Margaret could make a living from her handcrafts which could be sold in the local stores. With the increase in Donald's sales of boots and shoes, they had been thinking of setting up their business down on the lower level of the town.

Filled with enthusiasm, Chirsty pulled a warm coat over her dress and set off down the hill. A plan was beginning to form in her mind. Little Archibald ran along happily by her side. She started at the far end of the street which stretched along the waterfront, not sure what she was looking for.

Businesses and dwelling houses were jammed side by side along the main street, with the post office, Aros Hall and the new church right in the centre facing the fishermen's pier. Hotels and boarding houses catered for visitors who were lured to the Hebrides by tales of its scenic wonders.

Chirsty was certain that somewhere in this busy street she would find the perfect place for Donald to set up his business. A small building beside the post office caught her attention. The windows were blocked off and it was urgently in need of a clean.

A narrow lane ran alongside the building leading to the rear of the post office. Chirsty opened the door of the post office and went inside. Maggie Black was busy with a customer then turned to welcome Chirsty with a smile.

"How are the Argyll Terrace cottages working out?" she asked. "I've seen your mother from time to time and she seems most contented with life here in Tobermory."

"Our family has settled in really well and soon there will be another infant to enjoy the new dwelling.

"Donald is very busy with his shoe making but I feel he would do even better if we could find a place here in the town. Do you know if anyone is using the small hut beside the post office?"

Maggie Black explained that it had previously been used as a store room but was now vacant "apart from mice and spiders".  She took a key from a hook behind the door and offered it to Chirsty. "Why don't you take a look and see what you think? I warn you that is quite dismal at the moment, but could be improved I am sure."

Chirsty took the key and inserted it in the rusty lock. It resisted at first but then the door opened with a reluctant squeak. The interior was dark but as her eyes became accustomed to the gloom, Chirsty could see a large room with a long wooden table and a doorway which obviously led to a second room at the back. Two windows looked out onto the street but were covered with board.

She felt a surge of excitement. There was twice as much space as in Donald's present workshop and she knew it wouldn't take much to brighten the interior. She locked the door and returned the key to the post mistress. "If it is available I will bring Donald down to have a look. It looks ideal for what we have in mind."

Mrs Black was pleased to be able to help. It was a refreshing change to see a family wanting to build up their business in the town and not be heading off to greener pastures. She promised to have the information ready when Donald called. "Good luck to you," she said.

By the time Chirsty reached the Back Brae she was quite out of breath. She went straight out to the work shop where Donald was carrying out some shoe repairs. "I have found the perfect place for you to expand the business." She told Donald about the empty hut located in the best part of town, right beside the busy post office. "If you set up your workshop down there I'm sure you would soon need to hire some help."

Donald wasn't so sure. There were hardly enough hours in the day to carry out his present work load and renting a building would soon eat into the profits.

"I'll take a stroll down there and have a look," he promised. Chirsty's excitement was very

181

contagious. Their son John had just come in from school and was keen to take a look at the building so it wasn't long before father and son were off down the road to the village. "Your mother has some wild ideas young John, but believe me, we would be wise to humour her."

# Chapter 27

For Catherine and Neil Maclougas, life as they knew it was about to change. When Neil next called at the shipping office the clerk welcomed him and shook his hand. "Mr Maclougas, I'm pleased to inform you that you and your family have been accepted as immigrants by the New Zealand Company."

Neil took the papers with a trembling hand. He glanced at the first words on the document. "There must be some mistake," he gasped. "You have our name as McDougall. Surely these papers are meant for another family."

"There has been no mistake sir. It is a common policy for names to be simplified when you go to live in a foreign land."

Neil was startled. He knew that McDougall was an alternative name for Maclougas but had never used it himself. "I suppose that is a small price to pay for a new start."

"You will find a list of all that is required and you must be here three hours before sailing time on the given date. Good luck to you." The clerk shook Neil's hand firmly then turned to attend to the next man waiting in line.

With less than two weeks until departure, Neil knew there was no time to lose. First he would visit Catherine's family to share the news, then he would buy two cabin trunks at the hardware store before returning to his family.

There would be limited space on the ship but the family owned few belongings. Clothing and warm blankets would be a necessity as well as cooking equipment, a few household items and books for the children.

Neil's head was in a whirl as he walked up the steep track to the upper village. He thought he would talk to Donald McArthur before breaking the news to Catherine's parents.

As it happened, Chirsty was the first to greet him as he reached the Argyll Terrace cottages. She welcomed Neil into the house and brewed him a pot of tea. Neil looked around again at the sturdy dwelling which was a far cry from the dismal huts they had occupied on Ulva. "You have done well for yourselves. I have come with exciting news. Our family is set to make the long journey to New Zealand."

Chirsty gasped in astonishment. It had come as no surprise to learn that Alexander and Sally were planning to leave and she had always thought that young Hugh would be accompanying them. But Catherine and Neil and all the children? It was almost too much to take in.

"You do surprise me, brother-in-law. What does my sister think about making such a journey?"

"I have only just found out that we have been accepted by the New Zealand Company, but we have discussed the matter and Catherine has always indicated that she would support me in

184

my decision." Neil sounded confident but knew that his wife had mixed feelings about leaving her family and familiar surroundings.

Chirsty was dumbfounded. "I must call Donald and you can tell him the news. Our parents have just found out that Alexander and Sally are to leave on the ship, but they will be even more upset to hear about your family."

Donald was also astounded at the news. He would like to make the journey himself, but the thought of taking a wife and young children along was a daunting prospect. "You have obviously given the idea a lot of thought and I admire your decision. You are a braver man than me."

"I know that Alexander and Sally will be overjoyed that you will be travelling with them, and Sally will be of great comfort to Catherine." Chirsty tried to make light of the situation, but wondered how her parents would react, especially now that old Archibald was poorly.

She knew that they would need a great deal of support once the families had left. Donald had reacted favourably to the idea of moving his business down to the town, so this could prove to be a welcome distraction.

"I'd advise you not to tell our parents today," Chirsty said. "Let Donald and I discuss some ideas with them and find the right time to give them the news."

185

"I would be most grateful. Now I will go back and let Catherine and the family know what is to happen. I need to buy some cabin trunks and we are in for a busy few days sorting out what we can take along."

Chirsty promised to help provide anything the family needed. Between them they could surely send them away in style. Her daughters had dresses and skirts they no longer wore and she could spare a garment or two.

After Neil left, Chirsty hugged her husband. "Thank goodness I am not the one sailing away to goodness knows where. It looks as though it will be up to us to give my parents a comfortable life."

They sat around the table for a time, formulating a plan to increase their trade, a plan that would involve old Archibald and Margaret.

*******************

With a week to go before sailing, Alexander and Sally were still carrying out their duties for Francis Clark. During their time off they were gathering the items they would need to pack in the large trunk.

"I can't believe that Johanna Clark has been so generous. Look at this gown she has given me, and only yesterday it was two skirts and a blouse." Sally held up the clothing for Alexander to admire.

"I suppose she has more dresses than one person can wear in a lifetime, but it will be a great start for you in the new land." Alexander was grateful at the interest shown in their future. He had also received several items of clothing and a number of hand tools which would be put to good use when they arrived.

They would stay in Tobermory for two days, where they would be able to finish their preparations before their departure.

"I think it is safe to say that Hugh has changed his mind and will remain in Salen for the time being. So it will just be ourselves against the world," Alexander gave Sally a hug. "But with more than 200 souls on board the ship there are sure to be many familiar faces."

Sally was cheered that so many families from Mull would be sailing and was sure they would look out for each other in their new home. She realised that life on board the ship would not be easy, with males and females sleeping in different parts of the vessel. But there would surely be many chances to be with Alexander during the 100 day journey.

*******************

With the information that Neil and Catherine were to leave on the great ship Chirsty and Donald realized that they would be left to care for

Chirsty's parents. Hugh and Mary would be living a short distance away in Salen but unless they could persuade other members of the family to return to Tobermory, it would be up to them.

Donald had checked out the small shed down beside the post office and thought it would be worthwhile to move the bulk of his business down there. "If it doesn't work out then we will return to the back house which will be used in the meantime to store leather," he said.

The following day Chirsty went next door to tell her mother about their plans. Margaret was still distraught that Alexander and Sally were leaving for New Zealand and Chirsty noticed that old Archibald was sitting in the chair beside the fireplace.

"Come father," she said. "I have great news for you. Donald and I are to move our shoemaking business into the main town and you are going to help us."

"What do you mean, Chirsty? What can we do to help you?" Margaret was puzzled at Chirsty's enthusiasm.

"It could mean that you will have an outlet for your handcrafted scarves and hats. There will be space there for you to sell your wares."

Margaret took some convincing but in the end she was persuaded to visit the small store down on the waterfront. Chirsty borrowed the key and opened the squeaky door. They were taken aback

at the dust and grime but once the windows had
been cleared she could see that there was scope
for a new industry to be created.

Margaret was impressed. "Imagine having space
to display my craft and maybe find room for
others to sell their goods as well. You have done
well, Chirsty. I can see us surviving even without
Archibald's income from the lobster boats."

"It is a whole new life for us, mother. Together
we will survive in Tobermory."

Margaret didn't really know what Chirsty was
aiming at. She had got used to the idea of one of
her sons emigrating to New Zealand but she
would have so many family members around her
that she would hardly be troubled by it.

"Do you think people would buy my goods? I
would have to buy in some supplies and not rely
on the wool I am able to collect from the
brambles."

They locked the door of the building and
Chirsty returned the key to the post mistress. As
they passed a wooden bench, Chirsty stopped.
"Sit down, mother. There is something you don't
know. Neil and Catherine are taking the children
to New Zealand. Neil showed me the
confirmation today and he has gone home to
break the news to my sister."

The two women sat with their arms around each
other's shoulders. "Oh no, not the little ones,"

189

Margaret gasped. They sat for some moments as Margaret realized the enormity of the news.

Maggie Black stood on her doorstep and watched the scene unfold in front of her. She had seen it repeated many times over the past weeks as the last families were being signed up for the long journey. Excited husbands looking for a better life, wives unsure about what was ahead of them, and parents, broken hearted at seeing the strands that bound their families torn apart.

She sighed and went inside. It would be a good thing when the day came and the giant ship sailed away, leaving the rest of them to get on with their lives.

# Chapter 28

All over Tobermory there was an air of excitement. The hotels and boarding houses were full to overflowing as people converged on the town to see the tall ship out in the bay. Many were drawn by curiosity while others, such as Archibald and Sally were to spend their last two days sorting their belongings into the trunk. They knew that once on board, they would take out the clothing and bedding they would need for the journey and the trunk could be locked and placed in the hold.

Margaret had decided to make the best of the situation. Even though her heart ached there was little she could do about it. "You seem to have enough dresses. Miss Clark was most generous."

"I know. Three months is a long time but the space we have on board is limited. I will keep the best gowns for when we arrive. "Do you think that Alexander has enough trousers? And surely he won't be wanting that old hat." Sally held up a ragged helmet that had seen better days.

Margaret laughed. "He has owned that hat for many a year. I'm sure there is space for it."

Catherine and Neil had arrived the day before and the two cottages were brimming with people and luggage. Chirsty had found some dresses for Catherine to try and the children raced around clutching the skirts and blouses that had been worn by Chirsty's daughters.

Hand woven shawls and thick wool blankets as well as a set of table linen had been carefully placed in the trunks.

Neil and Alexander were quite bewildered by all the activity and sat outside with old Archibald who silently sucked on his pipe. "Sally and I are overjoyed that you are going to be with us. We were disappointed that Hugh changed his mind, but he may persuade his new bride to join us once we are settled."

"Your Sally will be a great help to Catherine, I am sure. In fact, we would not have considered it without your support." Neil looked across at the younger man and knew they would be good friends as well as brothers-in-law.

Archibald said nothing but watched the men as they talked. He had made the move from Ulva to Tobermory and that was as far as he was likely to travel.

A special service had been arranged in the church to farewell those who were leaving the next day. Muffled sobs could be heard as the minister bid them a safe journey and God speed across the waters.

Chirsty had organized a meal for them afterwards and Hugh and Mary made the journey from Salen to say their goodbyes. Hugh felt a surge of envy as he would dearly love to be travelling too. Mary watched him anxiously, but said little. She was so pleased that they were not leaving but knew that Hugh was far from happy.

As the sun set in the west that night, Margaret and Archibald walked to the seat at the end of the street and sat for a time watching the last rays sink below the sky line, the great ship silhouetted against the orange sky.

"Tomorrow will be a sad day but the young ones seem quite excited about the future. They will see many a sunset before they reach New Zealand." Margaret was subdued.

"When the moon is full and the sun rises each day, we will think of them. They will always be in our hearts." Archibald replied. "But now we must get some sleep as tomorrow will be a very busy day."

********************

Tobermory Bay was the scene for the biggest moment in its recent history, as the people clamboured onto the wharf with their luggage which was to go onto the great ship.

Margaret stood with her family on the jetty. Her daughter Catherine, who was keeping check of the children, and son Alexander, talking to his father.

Young Sarah was silent. She looked up to her grandmother. "I will always miss you," she said, the silent tears falling down her face. "But every time I have the chance to sing, it will be for you."

Then it was time for the women and children to board the boat. Catherine hugged her mother. "This is so hard. But I really think it is for the best. Look at all the people from Mull who will be living with us on the new land. We will be able to form our own community there."

"You go with our blessing, my dear. I know great things will come of this. Now go, and God be with you."

Sally was next to give her a hug. "I will help Catherine with the children, never fear. They think it is a great adventure." She allowed herself to be helped onto the small boat which was by now full of women and children. The boat pulled away from the shore and most of the women were silent. But then the wailing began. The sound eerily filled the bay.

Neil and Alexander waited on the jetty. They heard the sound and wondered how to react. The townspeople were quiet too as they realized the enormity of what they were witnessing. More than 200 of their people were leaving for places unknown.

But then the boat returned and it was the men folk who were to be ferried to the great ship. Alexander hugged his mother and grabbed his father by the hand. "We will make you proud. Neil and I will help create a new Scotland on those far off shores."

With that he stepped aboard the boat and waved to his family. The people of Tobermory were silent as the last of the passengers left their shores.

The crowd drifted silently away from the shore. From the look-out in Argyll Terrace the tall ship could be seen still anchored in the bay. A little after midnight it was escorted out into the open sea with most of the passengers standing on the decks to bid farewell to their homeland.

# Chapter 29

The next few days were busy ones for Chirsty and Donald. The building beside the post office was cleaned out and made ready for its new life as a cobbler's store. The windows were uncovered and glass fitted into the old wooden sills.

Curious onlookers poked their heads around the door to see what was going on and the news was soon being spread around the town.

"Come back next week and you will be in for a surprise," Chirsty promised. Donald's shoe-making gear was carefully unloaded from a cart and set up in the new premises. There were two long tables close to the door where shoes and boots could be displayed, and tall shelving behind the work area where the repaired footwear would be ready for collection.

It was decided that old Margaret would accompany Hugh and Mary back to Salen and help them move into their cottage. With so much to occupy her, she would have little time to grieve for her family who were out on the ocean.

Mary was delighted with her new home. There was a large kitchen, living area and two small bedrooms on the lower level as well as an attic above. There was no shortage of furniture as the inn keeper had supplied a table and benches and Mary's family had donated beds and blankets.

A trip to the hardware store produced pots and pans, and the contents of the wedding chest revealed a treasure trove of household items which Mary had collected before she was wed. "Our wedding guests were most generous. Hugh will need to put up more shelving to hold all this."

"You are very fortunate to have so many fine plates to display. We will help Hugh with the shelving when he returns." Margaret was intrigued at the variety of dishes being unpacked from the chest. Many were odd plates and jugs from the inn which Mary had saved from being thrown in the rubbish.

She could see why her daughter-in-law had been loathe to travel to New Zealand. There was no way she could have taken half her belongings with her.

Hugh seemed happy enough as he returned with the lengths of timber for the shelving and proceeded to fix it in place.

"There is plenty of space for us and we could take in a lodger to help pay the rent," he said. "But in meantime we will fix up the second room for anyone who cares to pay us a visit." Hugh had felt envious when his brother stepped onto the boat without him, but the sight of his new wife setting up such a pleasant home made him realise how fortunate he was.

197

"You are very lucky to have such a caring bride," his mother said, as she sat and watched them arrange their belongings. "Now, perhaps we should try out the cooking stove and prepare a meal." The fire was soon lit and the cooking pots put to good use. Alexander poured them all a mug of ale and they settled down to talk about the wedding and Donald and Chirsty's plans for the new cobbler's shop.

No mention was made of the 200 souls off the coast on the great ship.

**********************

The next day Hugh and Mary set off to work early and Margaret was left in their cottage. Of course, it was not new to her as her sister Ann had lived there many years before with her husband John MacDonald. She recalled visiting when her sister, who after having trouble conceiving, was raising a difficult child. Their son Charles had recently vacated the cottage and it was great that the family connection remained strong.

Margaret tidied up the interior and then went walking around the friendly little village. The waterfront was busy and the few stores were thriving. She wandered into the old church and sat for a time recalling the family events that had been held there. She thought about her parents who had been buried from here and anticipated visiting the graveyard at Pennygown on her way home where many of them rested.

Not wanting to outstay her welcome, Margaret decided she would return to Tobermory the next day. She knew that Donald and Chirsty would need help with establishing their new store on the waterfront and she looked forward to setting up the goods, ready for sale.

With all their wedding gifts and Mary's collection of china on display, the cottage looked very habitable. She hoped that Hugh would soon get over his disappointment about not leaving with his brother, but she felt that he seemed to be perfectly content with his lot.

********************

Margaret caught the early morning coach to Tobermory but insisted on stopping off at Pennygown graveyard on the way past. The driver was not in too much of a hurry and waited while Margaret went into the enclosure and found the monument for her family. It was very close to the walls of the old chapel and she stood for a moment in silent prayer. Then she rejoined the coach and set off along the road past Craignure and back to Tobermory where her family was waiting.

199

When Margaret arrived in Tobermory she went straight to the new cobbler's shop to see what changes had been made. "You are back early, mother," Chirsty said. "But we have made good progress. Come and see what we have done." She led her mother into the building which was now looking bright and cheery with the new shelving and paint work.

"These are the tables where your goods will be displayed. I'm sure you will sell enough to make a good living."

Margaret could hardly believe how much had been achieved. "I hope you haven't overdone it, my dear. I will have to work really hard to fill those shelves and maybe other women would like the chance to sell their work." She hugged her daughter and then took her leave. She needed to catch up with Archibald and fill him in with the news.

Archibald was asleep in a chair near the stove when Margaret returned to their home. He woke with a start as she entered and looked up in surprise. "We weren't expecting you back so soon. But it's good to see you, my dear." He rose stiffly and held out his hand to take Margaret's bag.

"I thought it best to let the young ones have their new home to themselves. That young Mary has gathered together enough household goods to fill two houses, I swear. I think that our Hugh is feeling quite bemused by the whole thing."

"At least it's taking his mind off travelling to New Zealand," was Archibald's reply. "Donald and Chirsty have been busy as well. They want me to spend time looking after the store while Donald works on his boots and shoes."

"The store is looking very grand and now I need to gather up enough stock to fill the tables." Margaret was eager to get busy on this new project. She knew of a number of women who would be keen to have somewhere to display their wares.

Finding a large cane basket she began to fill it with woven shawls and smaller items, but she knew she would need help from her friends. She wasted no time in visiting Mary McNeil who had been such a tower of strength during the children's visit for the Ceilidh. She needed to return the dress that Sally had borrowed for the wedding and there was plenty of news to share with her friend.

Mary McNeil was surprised to see Margaret McDonald looking so cheerful. She knew that a short time ago she had been devastated at the departure of the ship to New Zealand but she appeared to have bounced back into a positive frame of mind.

"So much is happening, my friend. I scarcely know where to begin," she said as Mary heated the water for a pot of tea. The two sat and caught up on all the news and Mary said she would help to gather supplies for the new store.

"I know there are several women capable of creating goods for sale. It would be a source of income for them, and Donald and Chirsty will need help organizing the supplies and keeping up the book work."

By the time Margaret returned to the cottage, Chirsty and the children were back and it was time to prepare the evening meal. Chirsty was interested in the news of Hugh and Mary's cottage and laughed when she heard about the trunk full of goods that had been collected. "No wonder she wasn't keen on travelling across the sea. She would never have been able to take everything with her." She stopped suddenly, not wanting to mention the ship, but her mother did not seem to mind the reference. Perhaps her plan to fill her mother's time was going to work.

# Chapter 30

Back in Salen, Mary and Hugh were sitting together at the new table eating the meal that Mary had prepared. The cottage looked very bonny, with the shelving completed and the plates and jugs displayed. Mary had taken great pains to dress in a becoming fashion. She wanted Hugh to feel content and not dwell on the fact that his brother and sister were somewhere out on the high seas.

Now that they were alone in their new dwelling, Hugh was also hoping that his marriage would at last be consummated. Each night they had lain together but there had always been someone close by through the thin walls and Mary had not been keen to give herself freely to him.

Their love making had involved a great deal of kissing and fumbling, complicated with clothing and sheets, but Hugh knew that his wife was still a virgin. They ate their meal and enjoyed a jug of ale then walked together along the quiet street as it was still daylight and too early for bed.

With the sun setting in the western skies, darkness was soon upon them and back in the cottage, Hugh steered Mary towards the bedroom and began to undress her slowly. Once down to her underclothes, she lay on the bed and covered herself with a sheet while Hugh took off his clothes and settled beside her.

She did not resist as he kissed her tenderly, then with more feeling and drew her hand towards his hardness. Before she knew it, Mary realised Hugh was on top of her, urging her not to resist him. Her legs parted enough for him to penetrate her, causing her to gasp with pain.

In a few moments, it was over and Hugh rolled away, leaving her feeling sore and confused. They lay together in silence, his arm around her body. She lay still while he snored softly in her ear, but it was some time before she fell asleep.

******************

Alexander and Sally were settling well into shipboard life. Once the ship left the coast of Scotland, land was in sight much of the time as they sailed on the Atlantic Ocean, heading away from the continent of Africa, then the current took them close to South America where they glimpsed the houses on the shore and passed many fishing boats lashed together like rafts, each carrying a three cornered sail.

The passengers had been assigned messes where their food was served and they took it in turn to bring the cooked food to the table and wash the dishes. This was not as easy a job as it sounded, as Alexander found out when he was almost washed away by a rogue wave as he crossed the deck with a plateful of beef.

The group was a cheerful one, setting themselves up as comfortably as possible, using cabin trunks as seating and sharing the tin plates, cups and cutlery that was available.

The women were all sleeping together, with Catherine and the children sharing with Sally, while the men were quartered in a different area of the ship. So far the seas had remained calm with little to trouble the passengers.

During the day the children, who numbered almost 100, were brought together for rudimentary lessons, supervised by a school master. There were few facilities for learning and it was a difficult task to occupy so many children of all ages.

Sally found herself being drawn in to help with the youngsters and devised simple games to keep them busy. A concert was planned for later in the week and performers were being sought. There was no shortage of fiddles and accordions and several singers had put their names forward.

Catherine had her hands full taking care of the little ones so it was left up to Sally to encourage young Sarah to volunteer. "Go on Sarah. You know you can do it," she urged. But Sarah was shy and hung back. Without her teacher, she had little confidence in her ability.

As the time for the concert drew nearer, she began to listen in to some of the rehearsals and without realizing it, one day she began to sing

along. "You have a very fine voice, my dear."
One of the fiddle players had been listening. He
started to play a simple melody and encouraged
Sarah to join in.

Soon people had gathered in a circle and as the
song ended they cheered heartily. Sarah blushed
and would have rushed off if Sally hadn't stopped
her. "The people loved you. Such a gift should
not be neglected."

The concert organiser was quick to notice and
came over with a sheet of paper in his hand. He
wasted no time in writing Sarah's name on the
list.

The young man who had played the fiddle spoke
to Sally. "Is this talented young lass your
daughter?" Sally had to explain the relationship
and they arranged for him to meet Catherine and
Neil and seek permission for their daughter to
perform.

"Some of the items may be a little bawdy, but
I'm sure that young Sarah could be
accommodated early in the programme."

The weather had remained fine and the seas
calm, but as they rounded Cape Horn and entered
the Indian Ocean they encountered the westerly
ocean drift and the winds were strong. Many of
the passengers took to their bunks as sea sickness
became rife.

Alexander sought out his wife and they
sheltered together for a time. "This is going to be

the worst part of the trip I fear," Alexander said as they were rocked from side to side. "But we are making good progress and so far we are all well."

"I do miss you, my husband. I can't wait to get onto firm land and be together again."

"That day will be here before we know it. Then we will make our way to our land and begin our new life."

"I'd better go back and check on Catherine and the children. So far they have not been affected by the rough conditions, but they may need some fresh air. It is far from pleasant in the women's quarters." Sally grimaced at the thought of going back into the crowded environment but knew she must do everything she could to help her new family. That was the only way they would survive in the days ahead.


******************

Back in Tobermory, Chirsty was busily setting up the cobbler's shop but at the same time she often wondered what her mother was actually thinking. Was she still pining for her children and grandchildren who were somewhere out on the ocean?

"Tell me Donald, what do you think? My mother never mentions the souls who have left our shores. I think about them all the time."

Chirsty had visions of her sister Catherine and the others all at the mercy of the seas.

"It seems that most of the voyages are smooth and after three months the passengers arrive safe and sound." Donald tried to reassure his wife who was beginning to bloom with her pregnancy.

During the day, Donald now worked down in the village and old Archibald was usually on hand to tend to the curious customers who poked their heads in the door. The tables were laden with goods for sale as Margaret and Mary McNeil had been busy rounding up supplies from the women of the village.

Chirsty was more than happy at the success of the new venture and enjoyed nothing better than sitting outside the store and tending the long table which held an array of woven and knitted garments. Old Margaret would take over when it was time for Chirsty to pick up the children from school and Archibald spent many a long hour sitting in his favourite chair and chatting to the customers.

# Chapter 31

It was almost 100 days since the great ship had left Tobermory and life on board had become somewhat tedious. The children were bored and the women anxious about what conditions would be like in their new land.

Alexander and Neil were standing by the rail when they got the first glimpse of land. A wide smile broke out on Alexander's face. "Neil, my friend. We have arrived safely and our new life can begin." The two men clutched each other for a moment and Neil had to look away as the tears threatened to fall.

They could see many hills, but none seemed very high. By the time they reached the heads most of the passengers were on the deck, all anxious to view their new land, but when the ship heaved to for the pilot to come on board, they were sent below till the anchor was dropped.

"When will we be there?" The children were running around in a frenzy, but they still had a long wait as it was not until the next day that the steam tug arrived to tow them into Port Chalmers. Much of the luggage had been brought up onto the deck the night before ready to be unloaded, and a number of passengers had to sleep on bare boards that night as they had thrown their mattresses overboard, thinking they would soon be on shore.

There was great excitement the next morning when two lighters came alongside to take the luggage. Then another delay until the tide rose, and at one o'clock the whistle was blown for everyone to board the steamer. Three hearty cheers went up as the steamer moved away and it took an hour before they reached the new town of Dunedin where a large crowd had gathered on the waterfront to welcome the new arrivals.

There was some consternation when they first stepped on land as the single women  were directed to the barracks but the men and families were left to fend for themselves.  Alexander and Neil were given two canvas tents and a space to pitch them in a field and they soon set themselves up with their cabin trunks acting as seats and tables.

Many of the newcomers were heading off to the gold fields as the promise of riches had lured them to try their luck, and Dunedin had become crowded with a high incidence of petty crime and violence, stimulated by alcohol.

Alexander and Neil set off to find food and were dismayed at the lack of public hygiene and the resulting smell of the streets. "We will be off to settle our land as soon as it can be arranged," Neil vowed, as they returned to their families with a few basic supplies.

They had managed to find a number of thin straw-filled mattresses and someone had set a fire on the edge of the field where they could heat their food.

Catherine was exhausted but the children thought it was all a great adventure. They unpacked their few belongings and laid the rugs on the mattresses.

"Welcome to New Zealand, my love. It's not exactly paradise but soon we will be standing on our own patch of earth." Alexander held Sally tight as they gazed out towards the distant hills.

*********************

It was less than a week later that the men, having purchased a horse and dray, packed it with everything they would need for the 20-mile journey south. They had called at the land office and had been given the deeds and a map of their land entitlement, with Neil and Catherine just a short distance from Alexander and Sally's plot.

With two sturdy tents, their mattresses and enough food to last a few days, the families set off in buoyant mood. It was good to leave the crowded town behind them and head along the narrow, rutted road which was formed during the gold rush, towards the wide open spaces of the countryside. Most of the land was covered with low-growing scrub with a few patches of grassland where earlier settlers had begun clearing their plots.

211

After travelling over a large plain and through a narrow gorge, their destination lay ahead. A small settlement had been established at Milton and it was there that the families arrived just as dusk was setting in.

A small group came out to welcome them and it wasn't long before the tents were set up on a field and they were being offered food and drink by the townspeople.

"This is most welcome to be sure. We will rest tonight, then find our way to our properties in the morning." Neil was overwhelmed at the hospitality shown to them.

"We are always happy to see people from the old country and catch up on some news of home," the people assured them.

It was with great relief that Catherine and Neil settled for the night. "This place is much more civilized than I imagined," said Catherine. "There are many fine people here and I am sure they will help us to settle in."

"It is probably best if you and the children remain here for a short time while Alexander and I go ahead to claim our land. I believe it is a short distance from here but we have no idea what we will find." Neil wanted his family to be close to the small settlement where they would not be alone.

Catherine sighed. It was so long since they had had a permanent roof over their heads, but she could see the sense in Neil going on alone. "I will rest here in good company," she agreed.

When Alexander put the proposal to his wife she was adamant that she would accompany him to their allotment. "The weather is mild and we could sleep out in the open if necessary." Sally had waited this long and was not going to be left behind.

"Very well. We will take a small tent and bedding and load up the dray with enough food and drink to last a week. Then Neil can come back and collect his family if conditions are suitable."

There was no way that Alexander wanted to be separated from his wife and tonight they would sleep together as they had done for the past week, curled up in each other's arms.

********************

Life in Salen had fallen into a pattern for Hugh and Mary. With the cold winter conditions, Hugh would travel up onto the hillsides to check the sheep but usually returned home each evening as the lambing season was some way off.

Although he said little to Mary, his thoughts were often with his brother Alexander and he wondered how the long sea voyage had treated

213

them. How he would have liked to be part of the great adventure.

"It is more than 100 days since my brother left these shores. They should probably be in New Zealand by now and seeking out their allotments."

"You are probably right. I wonder what their accommodation will be like." Mary looked around their cosy dwelling, grateful that she was not living in some God forsaken place. "Now sit yourself down and I will serve a meal." She bustled around, dishing the food onto two plates and setting them on the table.

"I think I would like to go out to the tavern tonight and meet up with some of our neighbours," said Hugh, as he finished his meal. Mary had worked there most of the day but she was more than willing to accompany him. She always enjoyed the atmosphere and knew most of the patrons by name.

A short time later they strolled arm in arm along the cobbled street. The wind was bitterly cold and the tavern, with its roaring fire, was a welcome sight. Hugh was soon surrounded by his friends while Mary sought out the company of her former room mate Annie. She had good news to share and wanted her friend to be the first to know.

"You look very bonny, my dear," Annie was surprised to see Mary back at the tavern. "I'm so used to seeing you in the black dress and apron."

"It's good to get out and give Hugh a chance to catch up with his friends before the lambing season starts." Mary blushed. "And I think I may be with child."

"Wonderful news. Unfortunately I am not so lucky, although it's certainly not through lack of trying." Annie looked wistful. "Is Hugh pleased that he is to be a father?"

"I haven't told him yet, but I'm sure he will be delighted." Mary couldn't believe that she had conceived already as their love making was still spasmodic.

"Then I won't say a word until you have informed him." Annie gave Mary a hug and together they went to join the other women who sat near the fire where they exchanged gossip and a few tankards of ale.

"Have you had any news of Hugh's family?" Mary was asked. "How brave they are to travel so far into the unknown."

Mary agreed, and looked across at Hugh, hoping he had not regretted staying back on Mull. Imagine being pregnant in an uncivilised land. Giving birth was a frightening enough prospect right here in Salen.

Chirsty's pregnancy was now well advanced and she left the running of the cobbler's shop to her parents while Donald was kept busy with the orders and repairs.
Young Archibald was always waiting eagerly for his brother John to return from school and they would play together in the back alley behind the cottages.

Ketty and Margaret were still sleeping at their grandparents' house but had chores to carry out before they were able to go off and have time to themselves.

Chirsty took the opportunity to rest whenever she could, but she knew she had dinner to prepare and washing to fold. As she looked at her lively family, she couldn't help wondering how her sister Catherine was managing without family support.

She still refrained from speaking about them to old Margaret and Archibald but they too must be wondering how Alexander and Catherine were coping. It would be great to receive news of their safe arrival, but unbeknown to them, the mail steamer had left Dunedin the day before the ship docked, so it would be many months before the next letters would arrive.

As she prepared the evening meal, Chirsty blessed the day she had married her husband Donald, who she had always been close to since their childhood on Ulva. Even in her pregnant state, she relished their nights together when she lay in his arms, protected from the world.

But now, old Margaret and Archibald came into view, followed by Donald, and it wasn't long before the whole family sat around the table to enjoy a wholesome meal. They tended to eat together these days as if to strengthen the family bonds that secured them.

# Chapter 32

It only took Alexander and Neil, with Sally accompanying them, just over an hour to reach the place on the map where they would find their land. The surveys had been done and the plots marked, and luckily there was an agent from the government in the area to help the new settlers identify their holdings.

Alexander found his boundaries first and he hugged Sally as they stood for the first time on their allotted land. Although it was covered with low scrub, it looked to be a level block of land with a hill at the rear.

Neil had a larger block as his children also had an entitlement, but it was just a short distance from where Alexander had set up his tent with Sally. Once again, most of the land was flat with a distinctive white rock which would eventually turn out to be a bonanza for the family.

As Neil took the time to explore his land, he came across a stream and a crude dwelling left behind by the gold diggers who had tried to find the elusive mineral on the property. The hut was made from baked mud with a timber roof and two rooms. "Look at this Alexander," he shouted. "It's every bit as good as our dwelling on the island of Mull. I'm sure we can bring Catherine and the children here without delay."

Alexander wasn't so sure. Indeed, it was a shelter of sorts, but far from any civilisation.

There was also the problem of earning a living. There was no way they could live for too long on a bare piece of land.

The young man who was working for the government was also curious as to how they would survive. "I could help you find employment if you need it," he said, when Alexander spoke to him the next day. "There is a landowner nearby who is hiring farm workers. I will give you his details and maybe you should call on him as soon as possible."

Although Alexander would dearly like to spend his days cultivating his own patch of land, he knew he would need an income, so he took the agent's advice and fronted up the next day at the large holding. He knew the owner was also from Scotland and would probably take him on.

When he heard that Alexander had worked for Francis Clark on the island of Ulva, James Green was very impressed. "You are obviously a good farmer. But I really need to teach you to become a ploughman. I'm sure you will be a quick learner. I could also find work for your wife."

Alexander returned to Sally who was waiting in the humble tent they had erected on their land. "We are very fortunate. Mr Green has agreed to employ us both and there is a small hut for us to live in. But I've never worked a plough in my life. Do you think I could learn the skill?"

"Of course you can, my husband. You will become a champion ploughman before you know it."

They embraced and set off to tell his brother-in-law the great news. Neil was keen to bring the family out to his allotment, but even with the small dwelling, he realized that it would be a hard existence for Catherine and the children. Maybe he should find employment back in Milton until they could afford to live on their entitlement. He knew they could come out to visit some weekends and stay in the hut whenever they wanted.

"I will leave you the horse and cart and go back to Milton tomorrow to seek work," Neil decided. "And I'll need to find somewhere for us to live."

They returned to Alexander's land where they lit a fire and heated up some food. It was a balmy evening as the sun set behind the distant hills. Sally retired to the tent, but the two men stretched out on the grass where they lay under the multitude of unfamiliar stars.

"I think we have found our little bit of paradise." Alexander sighed happily. "I'm sure that we have made the right decision."

******************

Back in Milton, Catherine was overwhelmed at the offers of help. She and the children were well set up in the tent, and there was a communal cooking fire as well as a good water supply close by. Sanitation was primitive however, with a bucket set up behind a shelter which was shared by several families.

Young Sarah turned her nose up at the idea of using the bucket, but after a while there was really no choice. Luckily it was emptied each day by a worker from the town council.

Catherine was impatient for Neil's return with news of their land. When he came into view, she hurried to meet him, anxious to hear all he had to tell her. "It is a fine piece of land, my dear, about five miles from here. Mostly flat with a hill and a small stream." When he told Catherine about the simple little hut on the property she couldn't believe their luck.

"We can go there and set up our home," she said, filled with excitement, but Neil was more cautious. "I don't think we could manage out there at this stage as I will need to find work and the children will have to go to school. But Alexander will come and meet us and we can go out and work on the land whenever time allows."

"Yes, I suppose that is for the best. Once you get a job we can move into a small house and settle the children into school." Catherine was happy to see Neil back and they made space for him in the tent which was becoming very crowded.

Little Mary Ann was now toddling around on her plump little legs and the older girls were busy keeping her in sight. Luckily there were several children from the ship now living in the tents and it didn't take them long to find the friends they had made on board.

The three girls and young John were all of school age and Catherine found that the school was a short distance from where they were camped. Sarah and Catherine would be in the senior class and John and little Margaret in with the juniors. With so many new children arriving, a new teacher had been appointed and an extra classroom was set up in the church hall until a new room could be built.

But now Neil had to find employment as their supply of money would soon run out. He went first to the town hall where the council office was based. There was a line of men ahead of him all newly arrived and in the same position as himself.

The clerk behind the desk took his particulars and told him to return the next day. The men heard that many workers were needed to construct a road just south of the town, which would form a main route from the city of Dunedin to the southern most part of the island.

"If you are not afraid of hard work, then come back tomorrow and we will take you on," the clerk promised.

In the meantime, Catherine had enrolled the children at the school. She met the head teacher and was impressed at his manner. He was interested to hear of Sarah's musical talent and promised to encourage her as best he could. John would be with the new teacher in the church hall while Margaret's teacher was a charming young woman with a friendly smile.

It was a very contented family that sat down to a meal that night. It looked as though they were well on their way to settling in their new land.

# Chapter 33

When Hugh heard of Mary's pregnancy he was delighted. "That is such good news, my love. We must visit the family in Tobermory and let them know as soon as possible."

Mary was a little shy about sharing the news so soon, but was pleased at Hugh's reaction. There were times when he seemed somewhat withdrawn and she was anxious to keep him happy.

The next time they both had a day off they decided to borrow a cart and drive around to Tobermory. They knew that old Margaret would be delighted at the news. It was late morning by the time they arrived in the village and the first place they stopped was outside the cobbler's store. Donald was hard at work in the background and old Archibald was seated near the door. He rose stiffly from his chair when Hugh and Mary came in sight and a wide smile wreathed his face.

"Your mother will be pleased to see you. She is up at the cottage right now."

Donald stopped his work to greet them and proudly showed them around his new store. "I am certainly getting far more orders since I moved into town," he said. "In fact, I may have to find a larger workshop and employ some help. I can't really expect my parents to be working so hard."

Hugh let the horse go in a small field at the bottom of the hill and it didn't take them long to walk the short distance to the Argyll Terrace cottage. Mary paused once in a while to catch her breath. "I'm not used to such a steep climb. We are fortunate that the streets in Salen are so level."

There was no-one at the first cottage but they could hear voices at Donald and Chirsty's house and young Archibald came running out to meet them.

Mary was surprised to see Chirsty's condition as she had not yet heard of her pregnancy. Margaret was busy tidying the rooms but came out and hugged Mary as they stood outside the cottage. "What a pleasant surprise, my dears. Come in and rest and tell us what has been going on."

Over the next few minutes they caught up on all that had been happening and when Hugh said they had some good news, Margaret knew what it was going to be. While several of her grandchildren were now many miles away, there were to be two more for her to welcome into the world.

"Well done my dears. I'm sure you will make great parents," she enthused. Chirsty was also delighted that there would be another grandchild for Margaret and this one could be the first to carry the family name. She was feeling large and uncomfortable as her bairn was due in two months' time.

"We must have some food and then I will be going down to the village to take my turn at the store," Margaret bustled around setting a pot of soup on the fireplace and placing a loaf of bread on a wooden slab on the table. Chirsty found enough bowls and cutlery and it wasn't long before the tasty meal was ready.

"This is a very happy day indeed," Margaret beamed. "To think there will be two more bairns to enjoy in just a few months." Chirsty looked at Mary and they smiled. It was good to see old Margaret so contented.

*********************

Although Archibald appeared to be coping with his work at the cobbler's shop, Margaret was secretly worried about him. She knew his joints were painful but the thing that concerned her most was that he often had to stop and catch his breath on the steep walk up the Back Brae to where they lived. His skin was quite flushed and it seemed as though his old heart was not coping as well as it should.

"I must try to get your father to visit Doctor MacColl, but I feel it might be a difficult task to persuade him. He's never really been ill in his life and he thinks he will go on forever." Margaret was sharing her concerns with Chirsty as they folded the washing that evening.

"There probably isn't a lot the doctor could do at his age. It's probably best to leave him be," was Chirsty's advice. She too had noticed that her father had aged over recent months but he seemed contented enough. Sitting at the door of the store was not exactly hard work after all that time on the lobster boat.

Hugh and Mary had returned to Salen and the younger children were settled for the night. The older girls were out with their friends but promised to be back before darkness fell. "Young Ketty is growing up fast. I think the lads will have their eye on her before very long."

"Aye, she is that. I noticed her talking with the McNeil lad the other afternoon. She is very mature for her age and is beginning to think like a woman." Margaret had noticed how quickly her eldest grandchild was growing up.

Ketty was indeed a bonny lass with long fair hair and a developing body. She was beginning to take pride in her appearance and had taken to checking out her reflection in the glass mirror which hung on the hook near the door. "I hate my hair. I wish it would curl like Margaret's," or "When can I have a new dress. This one is way too tight."

While her mother thought she was with her sister Margaret, Ketty was at that very moment

227

sitting on a grassy mound near the graveyard with her friend Charles McNeil. They were holding hands in a rather awkward fashion, each as shy as the other.

Charles was the grandson of Mary McNeil and a year older than Ketty who had recently celebrated her 15th birthday. They were both anxious to leave their school to seek work. "My father wants me to help out at the butcher's store but I would much rather be on the land," Charles was saying.

"If I leave school I'll be minding the children and helping around the house. Especially with another infant arriving soon." Ketty wasn't looking forward to all the extra work a new baby would bring.

"I'd really like to travel to Canada, or New Zealand like your family has done. That would be such an adventure." Charles' face lit up. "Imagine setting up in a new place with so much empty space and land for the taking."

"That would be quite a challenge. But we haven't heard from my folks yet and we don't know what conditions are like. I hear there are savages dressed in nothing but grass skirts. They are totally uncivilized."

"We should be getting back before we are missed." Charles stood up and dragged Ketty to her feet. "I don't think your folks would take too kindly to us being here alone."

"They'd be fine with it and anyway, we're doing nothing wrong." Ketty smiled at Charles as they set off down the hill to where the other youngsters were gathered.

**********************

It was late when Hugh arrived back from tending the stock and Mary was asleep in their bed. Although he was tired, Hugh would like to have woken his wife. Their love-making had been almost non existent since Mary had known of her pregnancy and he was growing impatient.

He resisted the temptation, however, and rolled over onto his own side of the pallet of straw that they shared. He needed to get up early in the morning to go back to the hillside to where the ewes were ready to lamb any time.

He may have to stay overnight in the crude little hut if he felt a birth was imminent. He lay awake for a time and thought about his brother who should be in New Zealand by now and perhaps settled already on his plot. Hugh had still not given up the idea of joining Alexander some time in the near future, but soon there would be a child to consider as well. He sighed a deep sigh and eventually fell into a troubled sleep.

229

# Chapter 34

The small town of Milton already boasted several stores as well as a Scottish church and the school. With the construction of the new road already underway, several new businesses were setting up close to the road away from the established town.

Neil joined a number of other keen new workers who were all pleased to have found employment so readily. "Once this road is completed, the old township will disappear," said one of the workers. "It would be a good time to invest in land down here if you had money to spare."

The other workers looked at him in astonishment. They were all down to their last few pennies and knew that every pound they made would be used to develop the land they already owned. Neil could see that the young man was talking sense, but he had no funds to spare for such an investment.

After Catherine had settled the children in their new school, she took time to explore the small settlement. There was quite a heated argument going on as she waited to be served in the general store. "I say the English church needs to be built down near the new road. That is where the settlement will develop." The customer was adamant.

"Nonsense. We all live up here on the hill. The settlement will always be up here."

"But the flour mill is on the lower level and doing a great trade I hear. The new farmers would be wise to lease their land out for growing wheat. It would give a quicker return than raising stock."

Catherine pricked up her ears. She would tell Neil what she had heard. The store keeper greeted her as she put her purchases on the wooden counter. "You are new here, my dear?" The woman was curious. She counted out the change which Catherine pocketed carefully, and admired little Mary Ann, who had a ready smile for everyone.

"Yes, we only arrived on the ship three days ago and my husband has found work on the new road until we can take up our allotment."

"The best of luck to you. We get so many travellers passing through to the gold fields. It is good to welcome new settlers to our town."

They spent some time in conversation before Catherine made her way back to the tent with her supplies. She passed a number of small cottages and knew they would need to find accommodation soon before the winter weather set in.

Once in a while she wondered how the family was faring back in Scotland. It seemed to be a lifetime away and so far, she had no regrets about making the move.

*********************

232

In spite of Chirsty's advice, Margaret was worried about Archibald who seemed to be getting weaker every day. She sought out Dr MacColl for advice, but his answer was much the same as Chirsty's. "At his age there is not much to be done. See that he rests and try to keep him occupied."

Spending time in the store each day certainly kept him interested in his surroundings, but climbing the steep hill back to the cottage was becoming more difficult. This was solved by the butcher who used a small pony cart to deliver meat to his customers.

"Your husband is most welcome to ride up the hill with me. I leave each afternoon around 3 o'clock." And so it was that old Archibald was hoisted up onto the cart each afternoon, "Just like a side of beef," he would say, arriving home in good condition just as the children were coming out of school.

Margaret and her friend Mary McNeil had done a good job of gathering up goods to be sold in the store. Crocheted garments, woven rugs and hand knitting were proving popular with the visitors from the mainland who came through the town from time to time.

"The women are very happy to be earning money from their craft, and Donald is being kept busy repairing shoes. He hardly has time to work

233

on new styles," Chirsty commented one afternoon. She was spending less time at the store as her baby's birth was imminent.

The children could be heard outside but when they appeared, Ketty was not with them.

"Where is your sister? She knows she has work to do before tea time." Chirsty was cross. There was a pile of washing to deal with and her mother had just returned from the village and had work of her own to carry out.

"Ketty? I'm not sure. She left the same time as we did." Margaret did not want to get her sister into trouble, as she knew that Ketty had gone walking with Charles McNeil.

"Well, you will have to help fold the clothes and put them away, as your sister isn't here to do it." Chirsty had enough to do with a meal to prepare and the younger children to supervise.

John took little Archibald out into the yard to play and Margaret shrugged her shoulders and set about the task. She knew she would have to take a bigger share of the work load once the new baby was born.

Charles had waited outside the school for Ketty to appear and the two went walking up the Back Brae towards the cemetery where they sat on a wooden bench which overlooked the bay. "My grandfather was drowned somewhere out in that sea," Charles said. "He perished in a wild storm. The fishing boat was never found."

234

"That is really sad." Ketty tightened her grip on Charles' hand. "Your father didn't follow in his footsteps and become a fisherman?"

"No, I don't think his mother would have allowed it. She wanted him safe and sound on dry land."

"My dad has always been a shoemaker, even when we lived back on Ulva. I remember the pile of leather and all his tools in the small croft where we lived. His new store is such a big improvement."

Charles admitted that he had never visited the small island of Ulva and was curious about it. "They say the owner has moved everyone off to make way for sheep."

"My Uncle Alexander was working for Francis Clark and he seems to be a good man. Our family met him at the wedding." Ketty could remember the hardship her family faced before coming to Tobermory. "The island couldn't support so many people. There are only a few farm workers employed there now as far as I know."

They chatted on companionably for a while, until Ketty realised that her mother would be looking out for her. "I'll be in big trouble if I stay much longer, but it's been grand talking to you."

Charles accompanied Ketty back to the corner of her road, then walked on down to his own home in the village beside the butcher's shop. His father was just on his way back down the hill with the pony and cart and he was able to catch a ride.

"Hop aboard young Charles. I have just delivered Archibald McDonald back to his cottage. He is good company and it is no trouble for me to help him out."

Charles realised that Archibald was Ketty's grandfather but didn't say that they had been together. Their friendship was best kept secret for now.

# Chapter 35

When Neil arrived back after his first day toiling on the new road, he was exhausted. "I thought life as a shepherd was bad enough, but digging out all those rocks is certainly hard on the body."

"We haven't even got a bath tub for you to soak in. Or a comfortable chair where you can rest." Catherine was concerned. It was all very well living in a canvas tent, but there were few home comforts, that was for sure.

The days were growing shorter and the nights cooler, so looking for a cottage to rent was becoming most imperative. Neil knew there were dwellings available, but he had little time to seek one out.

"It might be up to you to find us a new home. We should be able to pay the rent from my earnings." Catherine agreed. She knew that she had more time than Neil and vowed to look around the town the next day after she had dropped the children off at school.

She served a meal which they ate seated on their cabin trunks, their plates on their laps. The eldest girls were sent to the water pump to fill a bucket and wash the cutlery and plates, then they went off to seek out their friends.

Neil left for work early next morning and Catherine supervised the children as they dressed ready for another day at school. Once she had dropped them off she set out to make enquiries about accommodation. The general store seemed as good a place as any to start with and the store keeper welcomed her with a smile.

"Nice to see you back, my dear. By the way, my name is Annie Clegg. My family arrived two years ago from England and my father set up this store not long after we arrived."

"It's good to make your acquaintance, Annie. My husband started working on the new road yesterday and I am trying to find somewhere for us to live before the colder weather sets in."

"There are several houses available as many settlers have already moved onto their allotments. Have a look around the town and if you see an empty dwelling that could be suitable, come back and let me know." Annie Clegg was helpful.

Catherine hoisted little Mary Ann onto one hip and picked up her bag. She made her way carefully along the roughly paved road until she came to a street of narrow wooden houses, some with a small porch attached to the front. Several showed signs of being inhabited with smoke furling from their chimneys and others were closed up with little sign of life.

A woman was hanging washing on a clothes line and stopped what she was doing when Catherine walked by. "Are you looking for someone?" she enquired.

"I'm actually seeking an empty dwelling which my family could rent," Catherine said. "Do you happen to know which houses are available?"

"Most of the houses in this street are owned by the manager of the local bank. If you call and see him I'm sure he would be keen to help you."

Catherine thanked the woman and walked back towards the town centre. The bank occupied a small building on the corner of the street and she wasted no time in approaching the building and opening the solid door.

A stern looking woman sat at a desk near the entrance and a young man could be seen behind a glass shield at the counter. The woman looked up from her work and greeted Catherine. "How can I help you?" she queried.

Catherine explained that she was seeking accommodation and the woman pulled out a heavy folder. "There are a number of houses available at present, but it depends on the amount you can afford to pay."

"We have just arrived from Scotland and my husband has found work on the new road. We have been granted an allotment but need to be close to town until we save enough to cultivate our land and build a shelter there."

The bank clerk had heard this story many times but could see that the woman was genuine. She took down the details and raised her eyebrows a little when she heard that there were five children. "That was a brave thing to do, to leave your country with such a large family." Her face softened a little. "I will prepare a list of suitable properties with space for your children. If you call back tomorrow I can let you have the details."

Catherine felt very hopeful as she left the bank building. The houses were modest but sturdy with space for a garden. She walked back along the street again, mentally noting the empty houses. Some were in better condition than others, but even the most shabby were superior to their former cottage on Mull.

It was dark by the time Neil returned that evening so there was no chance to show him the dwellings. "I'm sure we will be content with a roof over our heads, no matter how simple. In fact, the one with the cheapest rent would be best." Neil was keen to save as quickly as possible so they could develop their own land.

They crowded together as they lay in the tent that night, but Catherine was sure tomorrow would see a change in fortune.

*********************

In the meantime, Alexander and Sally had settled into life on James Green's fine property. Most of the acreage was already in grass and

Alexander was surprised at the number of sheep grazing there. There were also two milk cows which Sally was only to happy to look after. Their hut consisted of one room with a fireplace set on the back wall where they could cook their meals and heat water.

Alexander had received instructions on how to use the plough. It was pulled by a horse, but was still heavy and awkward and he had to guide it in the right direction, but after a few false starts he was beginning to get the feel of it.

They decided to take the horse and cart into town on their day off and replenish their stock of food. Sally was also anxious to catch up with Neil and Catherine and see how they were faring. "I hope they have been as lucky as we have. They have many mouths to feed."

"Yes, I would like to be able to do more to help them, but we are just too far away." Alexander felt a little guilty that he was not on hand to help his sister and the rest of the family. He knew that Sally had been a great comfort to Catherine during the long sea voyage and they missed the presence of the children.

It was Sunday morning before they were able to return to Milton and they were full of excitement as they climbed onto the cart and set off along the rough, narrow track. "They say there is to be a new road through this valley before too much time has passed. Then it will be a quick trip back

241

to town." Alexander knew that one day their property would be just a short journey from Milton.

They climbed a steep hill covered with bush and from the summit they could see the town of Milton in the distance. It was spread over quite a large area, with the older settlement on the hillside and new developments down on the flat. They wound their way down the track and soon reached the camp ground where the new settlers had pitched their tents.

Andrew tethered the horse then set off in search of their family, which proved difficult as there were now several rows of tents all looking very much the same. There were a number of children playing on a vacant area and Sarah and Catherine were among them.

When they saw Sally and Alexander they rushed up to greet them, eager to tell them all the news. "We are already attending school and our mother has found us a cottage to live in." They dragged Sally over to their tent with Alexander following. Catherine heard all the excitement and came out to see what was going on.

"What a great surprise. Come into our humble home and tell us what you have been doing." She instructed the girls: "Go and find your father. He is off with the boys but can't be far away."

Catherine poured a cold drink of barley water from an urn and offered it to her guests. "As you can see we are living in a very simple manner, but I think we have found a house to move in to. I have to go back to the bank on Monday and finalise the arrangements."

A few moments later, Neil arrived with the boys in tow and filled Alexander in on all that had happened in the past few days. "I can't believe that I already have work and we have been promised a place to live. I'd rather be out on my own land, but for now everything is going better than we expected."

"That is great news, my friend. Sally and I have also been most fortunate. We are able to earn a living and at the same time, our property is close by and we can spend a little time there."

As the men talked, the women took the opportunity to walk through the town and although the stores were officially closed, Annie Clegg agreed to sell Sally a few items. "I know you can only come here on a Sunday, so I will have to turn a blind eye to trading on the Sabbath. We have attended church this morning so I'm sure the Lord will forgive me."

With a boxful of provisions, Sally returned to the camping ground. The children were eager to show their visitors the school and the cottage that had been promised to them. It was a little larger than the others and stood at the end of a narrow lane. It appeared to be somewhat neglected, but

Neil knew they could repair it and the rent was cheaper because of its condition.

They walked up the overgrown path and peered in the dirty windows. There seemed to be one large room with two smaller rooms on one side. A kitchen of sorts could be seen through a small window at the back. There was no cooking stove but an open fireplace with hooks to hang the pans. A tin tub on a wooden stand by the back door would have to serve as a wash room and a small lean to further down the path housed a deep hole with a wooden seat.

"Ooh, I'm sure there are spiders down there." The children were fearful, but their father reassured them that it was perfectly safe.

"We'll soon have this place looking like a palace," he said cheerfully, and Catherine agreed that it would be much better than living in a tent.

The day passed quickly and soon it was time for Alexander and Sally to return to the farm. They were pleased that Neil and Catherine seemed to have settled so well but knew it would be some time before they could start clearing their land.

"We must go by our own property. It's hard to imagine that we actually own it. I would dearly love to spend some time clearing a patch and planting a crop."

In the evening light their land stretched out before them. They knew there would be hours of work ahead of them to clear the bush and plough the land ready for a crop, and they were keen to make a start.

"Just think. We will build a dwelling from our own timber and grow our own food." Alexander looked around him, a contented smile on his face.

Sally shared his enthusiasm. Although she knew that the cold winter weather would soon be upon them and the days would be short, they had a lifetime ahead of them.

*********************

With the lambing season in full swing, Hugh was out on the hillsides from the crack of dawn until late into the night. There were times when he had to assist with a difficult birth, but most of the time it was just a matter of letting the ewes get on with the job.

Occasionally he would come across a sheep tangled in a thorn bush or a lamb that had fallen down a steep ridge and needed to be returned to its mother, but he had plenty of time to sit and ponder.

He was pleased that Mary was with child and his home was warm and comfortable, but he still envied his brother far away in New Zealand.

Mary was feeling well and able to carry on her work at the tavern. No-one apart from her friend Annie knew of her pregnancy and it was easy to hide her condition under the skirts and apron she wore.

She was kept busy, especially during meal times when there were hungry mouths to feed and empty tankards to fill. Sometimes the guests were noisy and boisterous, especially when they came from the ships docked at the wharf, but she was used to avoiding their advances.

"You cheeky thing. Don't you know that I'm an old married woman." She would smile and move away, going on to attend to the next customer. Mary enjoyed her work and wanted to carry on as long as possible. Her wages helped pay the rent on their cottage and she knew they would possibly need to take in a lodger once she was home looking after the infant.

She was weary by the end of the day, however, especially if she had to work into the evening. Then she would walk the short distance home and sit down in her favourite chair, waiting for Hugh to come home. On those occasions, she was usually able to bring him a ready cooked dinner from the kitchen which saved her having to prepare a meal.

She and Annie would eat earlier with the rest of the kitchen and serving staff. Tonight there was roast beef and plenty of vegetables and the cook smiled as she dished up a portion for Mary. "Your husband will be looking forward to his meal after working all day on the hillside. I will dish up a portion and leave it on the bench for you to take home."

Mary realised how lucky she was. She didn't imagine that Sally or Catherine, far away in New Zealand, would be so fortunate. They were no doubt struggling to cook for their men in the most primitive conditions. "Every day I thank my lucky stars that Hugh gave up the idea of travelling on the great ship," she confided in her friend.

"I wouldn't be too sure that he has actually forgotten the idea, but with the bairn due to arrive in a few months, he has certainly put the idea on hold." Annie knew that Hugh still hankered for the chance to live on his own land. Her own husband often spoke of it as well. "Maybe we'll all be living in New Zealand before too much time has passed."

# Chapter 36

It was a cool day in May when Neil and Catherine moved into the empty house in Milton. They opened the door and looked around and although there was a great deal of work to be done to make it liveable, it felt like a mansion compared to the crowded tent or the little stone cottage back on Mull.  It didn't take long to unload their few possessions, including the cabin trunks which they had brought out on the ship. The previous tenants had left behind a rough wooden table which Catherine scrubbed until the bare wood gleamed. They would find boxes for seats and their mattresses were placed on the floor of the two bedrooms.

"You older girls will have to sleep in the big room for now and give the little ones the bedroom. Neil and I will take the baby in with us." Catherine shared around the blankets and placed a linen cloth on the table.

Neil was doing his best to clean the small kitchen which consisted of a narrow wooden bench and a cupboard with shelves and a broken door. A few half-burnt logs had been left in the fireplace at the back of the kitchen which had a wide chimney to let out the smoke.

Sarah needed to use the outhouse but put it off as long as possible. "Wait outside the door for me," she urged her sister. "I don't want to fall down that deep dark hole."

Catherine was only too happy to oblige and followed Sarah along the overgrown track. A stray cat ran off as they approached the lean-to. "We've got a cat." Catherine shrieked with excitement. "We can leave out some food and try to tame it."

Sarah was not sure her parents would want them to share their precious food supply with a cat but it could be their secret in the meantime. It would be so good to have a pet of their own.

Neil sent the boys out to gather logs and small branches from the nearby bush. They soon came back with an armful each and combined with the dry wood which had been left in the fireplace, they managed to get a fire started. Catherine hung a pot of water from a hook and stood back taking in the scene.

She would boil some vegetables along with a pork bone which the storekeeper had given her and there would be enough to feed her family tonight. Tomorrow they would buy in some more supplies with the last of their savings.

They sat on the cabin trunks which were serving as seats as the meal was dished up on the long table. "I think we should join hands and thank the Lord for all our blessings." Neil was not normally a religious man, but tonight he was content with his lot. The small dwelling would provide shelter for his family until they were able to move onto their own land.

*********************

Alexander and Sally were kept busy working on James Green's farm, but every spare moment they got they were off to work on their own plot of land. They chose a flat area covered with low scrub and Alexander chopped while Sally carried away the branches until they had cleared a substantial area.

"We will buy some seed potatoes and corn next time we are in Milton," Alexander promised. "It will be easier to grow crops until we can fence the fields and plant grass for stock."

Any large logs were set aside to use for fencing when the time came and Sally had already chosen a site for the house they would build some day. It wasn't too far from the road on a gently sloping hill and it would be easy to form a track up to the site.

Alexander was becoming quite skilled at using the plough and Sally would follow behind and pick up the stones and small rocks which were loosened. These were stacked up to form walls which divided the open land into smaller fields.

There were two cows to milk each morning and night and Sally also churned the cream to make butter which was enjoyed by the farm workers who shared a mid day meal of bread, meat and pickle. At times James Green's wife cooked up scones or cakes as a special treat and once a week all the workers joined the Green family for a meal which was cooked in the back yard of the homestead. Two Maori workers would prepare a hangi earlier in the day. A fire was lit in a hole in the ground, then the food was placed in flax baskets which were set on steaming rocks and covered with wet sacks and earth.

Alexander and Sally discovered that chicken, pork, cabbage, kumara and pumpkin were delicious when cooked that way.

"We are very fortunate to have found such a good employer. Although we work hard, Mr Green treats us well and makes sure we get to enjoy the company of our fellow workers at the end of the day." Sally had met the wives of two of the other employees and they were becoming good friends.

Elsie and Belle were English and loved to tease Sally about her broad Scottish accent. "It's ye that have the accent," Sally would reply as she found the Yorkshire brogue difficult to understand. The women had arrived in New Zealand 12 months before and lived with their husbands in simple shacks on their own land.

Alexander and Sally had seen their plots and were surprised at how quickly the gardens had grown. Elsie had brought flower seeds with her from England and they were beginning to bloom, while Belle had planted carrots and swede as well as beans and potatoes.

"The weather will close in soon and they say snow may fall." Alexander was anxious that their small hut would be warm enough for winter. He stocked up on wood to keep the fire burning as the walls were thin and the wind seemed to whistle through all the cracks.

"As long as we have firewood we should be snug," Sally assured him. She had discovered that if you mixed a quantity of mud with water it formed a paste that hardened and could be used to seal the gaps. They had also been told to spread lime on the soil before planting their crops as it was proving to be excellent fertilizer.

"I can see the day that the farmers will be spreading the lime on their pastures. It could turn out to be a very valuable product in the near future," Alexander said.

Alexander had written to his family back in Tobermory and they were anxiously awaiting a reply. They often wondered how the old folk were faring, especially Archibald whose health had been failing.

"Chirsty may have a new bairn by now. She will have her hands full with so many children." Sally was envious. She suspected that she might be with child but it was too early to be sure. At least

252

the worst of the cold weather would be over
before the baby was born.

*********************

With Chirsty's baby close to being born, she
spent less time at the cobbler's shop and
Archibald and Margaret were happy to help out.
Margaret had set up a loom in the shop and spent
many hours working on the woollen scarves and
rugs which were popular with the customers.
Several of the other women were also selling
their hand-woven goods and knitted garments and
were pleased to be able to earn a few extra
pounds to supplement the family income.

Donald was kept busy with his shoemaking and
began to look around the village for larger
premises. "It would be grand if we could find a
house to live in down here in the town with a
workshop attached. It would need to be large
enough for you to share," he told Archibald.

He asked the other storekeepers to keep their
eyes open for a suitable property and each day he
would walk along the length of the harbour front
trying to find something suitable.

As usual it was the post office mistress Maggie
Black who came up with the answer. People
tended to share their news when they picked up
their mail and one morning she heard of a family

who were moving out to live in Oban. They were occupying a large house on The Breast with a storage shed attached. It backed onto the steep cliff below the upper village and was just around the corner from the post office.

Wasting no time, Donald found out who owned the house and paid the gentleman a visit. He knew that the children would have further to go to school each day but they were old enough to climb the Back Brae along with many other youngsters who lived down near the waterfront.

Donald was in high spirits when he returned home that night. Chirsty sighed as she heaved her body from the seat where she had been resting. "You seem to be in good spirits tonight, Donald. What news do you have?"

"How would you like us to move down to the lower village where there would be space for the family and your parents, and best of all, a shed attached which is perfect for a cobbler's shop."

Although she was happy with the two cottages in Argyll Terrace where they had been for such a short time, Chirsty could see the sense in sharing a home with old Archibald and Margaret. And to have the cobbler's shop attached would make life a lot easier.

"It would be quite a step for the children to go up to the school," she said. "But I guess they could manage. Our church is also up the hill and it would be difficult for my mother to make her way there.”

“We might have to look at going to the new church down in the village, but I feel that Margaret will make her way up the hill for many a year yet.” Donald could not imagine his mother-in-law missing a service while she still had the use of her legs.

As they shared a meal later that night, they discussed the idea with Archibald and Margaret who agreed that it would be more practical than living in the two cottages on the hill. “I think you should take the house and we can contribute towards the cost,” she said, knowing that she would be able to make more from her handcrafts if she was based in the town.

The children were excited at the idea as well. There was always something going on down in the lower village and they would be part of it.

# Chapter 37

On a stormy night about three weeks later, Chirsty's new son was born. He came so quickly he took everyone by surprise and old Margaret assisted with the birth before the midwife could be summoned. "A fine boy. John and Archibald will be happy to have another brother and he is to be named Donald," Margaret enthused.

Young Ketty had also been involved with the birth although the whole scene was enough to put her off becoming a mother for the time being. She was still seeing a lot of young Charles but was careful not to go too far when they were alone together.

"There will be plenty of time for that once we are wed," she would say when he urged her to lie with him. Now that she had witnessed the birth of her latest brother she hoped that childbirth would be a long way off for her.

Little Donald was a calm, contented child and although young Archibald was somewhat put out and at first and clung onto his mother's skirts to seek attention, he soon went off to play with the other children, who reluctantly included him in their games.

The house on the lower level was now empty and the family moved their belongings down the hill just a week after little Donald was born. Donald had already set up his cobbler's shop in the new premises and there was plenty of space for Margaret to display the increasing number of handcrafts.

With three large rooms on the lower level and a loft above, there was plenty of space for everyone in the new dwelling. An empty yard beside the house would soon be transformed into a garden and there was a small fenced area where the younger children could play.

Archibald and Margaret shared one of the rooms and took turns at looking after the shop while Chirsty was kept busy with the new baby and organizing the other children. Having her parents right there to help was a huge bonus and at times she wondered how her sister Catherine was coping so far away from family support.

It was an exciting day when a bundle of letters arrived from New Zealand. Maggie Black was almost as excited as they were as she handed Margaret the package and was keen to share the news from over the sea.

There were letters from Alexander and Catherine, and the older children had also sent along notes telling of their adventures.

"They appear to be settling down very well and have already started working on their land." Archibald was pleased to hear of their progress when Margaret read the letters to him. "So Alexander is now a ploughman. That is an excellent occupation."

257

The children were intrigued with the descriptions of their new land, with their school and particularly, their outhouse. Catherine's daughters had described in detail the experience of sitting over that long dark hole waiting for the spiders to jump out.

Although Margaret missed her family she knew they were happy and content in their new land.


**********************


Winter had now struck with a vengeance in the South Island of New Zealand with snow and sleet obliterating the landscape. The primitive shack where Alexander and Sally were living was barely adequate and they often sat huddled beside the cooking fire during the long winter evenings.

Sally had now confirmed her pregnancy and Alexander was anxious to upgrade their housing before the infant was born. Their employer was sympathetic and anxious to help them as much as he could. He realized that Alexander had become a valuable worker and Sally was also doing more than her share of the work.

When a larger cottage became available, James Green was only too willing to offer it to the couple. "You have proved to be good workers and I want you to be happy in my employment."

Alexander was impatient to begin building on their own land but knew that they would have to wait until he had saved sufficient capital. In the meantime they would be more comfortable in the new dwelling.

With the winter conditions, Neil and Catherine were no longer able to spend weekends on their property, but their life in Milton was more than tolerable. Work on the new road was progressing well and Catherine had made the simple dwelling as comfortable as possible.

The children had settled well into their new school and young Sarah was preparing for the annual concert where she was to sing a solo, accompanied by an orchestra which had been formed by local musicians.

"It is lucky that your cousins gave us some clothing before we left Scotland. I'm sure we can make something of these." Catherine dug deep into the cabin trunk and came up with a garment and shook it out. "I can remember seeing Ketty in this skirt. She must be quite a young woman by now."

At times Catherine wondered how her family was faring back in the old country. She was usually too busy to think about the past but sometimes the memories were strong. She felt a tug of nostalgia as she held the garments that had remained for so long in the trunk. Chirsty had been most generous as they were leaving and she held the skirt out to her daughter to try on.

Teamed up with a bright red sash and a simple white blouse, the blue skirt suited Sarah admirably and she knew she would look well on the night. "I am so nervous. I'm sure I will forget my words," she sighed.

"You will be great and we are all very proud of you," her mother assured her.

It was an excited family that crowded into the town hall the next evening. A fire had been lit in the small stove to warm the room and the seats and benches were soon filled. Several of the students were to give items and a number of adults had also been encouraged to share their talents. Many of the families were new settlers and the concert would be an opportunity to meet up and share their experiences.

As Catherine found a seat near the front of the hall and Neil joined the other men who were standing outside the door, the young people gathered with their classmates ready to shuffle up onto the stage. The pianist struck a chord and the crowd was hushed, as the schoolmaster welcomed everyone and introduced the first act.

A dozen or so anxious children filed onto the stage and faced the audience. They were the youngest pupils in the school and were all scrubbed and on their best behaviour. They managed to perform two simple songs and were ushered off to a great round of applause.

The older children were next and played a tune with bells, tambourines, two fiddles and a drum which had the audience tapping their feet with enthusiasm. Then they left the stage leaving young Sarah McDougall standing alone. The orchestra played a few lines and then the piano alone accompanied Sarah as she sang a Scottish melody, her voice filling the hall with a glorious sound.

Catherine gasped. Her daughter was giving a superb performance, with a maturity beyond her years. There was total silence as she finished, then the applause erupted. The audience rose to their feet and clapped and cheered, demanding an encore.

Sarah stood in the middle of the stage, her face red with embarrassment, but with a word from her teacher, she launched into another folk song, reducing many to tears as they were carried away by the familiar words and the plaintiff tune. It brought back memories of the land they had left so recently and reminded them of what they had left behind.

Catherine was surrounded by the other parents, as she wiped the tears from her eyes. Then she smiled. Her new friends were all around her. For a few moments the music had made them forget their shabby clothes and primitive living conditions. They were full of praise for her daughter and knew they had just witnessed a great talent.

Now it was time for the adult entertainers, but Sarah had outshone them all. It was a tired, but happy family that returned home that night. Neil was determined that everything would be done to help his daughter achieve her potential.

"I'm sure there will be a music teacher who can work with Sarah. Such a talent can not be wasted." He put his arm around Catherine's shoulders and drew her close as they helped the children into their beds and doused the candles.

# Chapter 38

Old Archibald sat in the armchair beside the shop door and surveyed the scene. The harbour was filled with small boats returning from their fishing trips and a number of sail boats ready to race in the bay.

He sighed as he thought of the way he had toiled over the years to make a good life for Margaret and the children. He held the latest letters from New Zealand to his chest. Although he couldn't understand most of the words, Margaret had read them over to him a number of times and he could picture his son out in his own fields and his daughter making a home in that far off place.

Alexander had sent the good news that Sally was with child and they were hoping to start building their own simple dwelling before very long. He had cleared a portion of the land and several of the other settlers had brought their ploughs along and helped till the soil ready to plant a crop.

"If I had my time over I would be out there helping the lad." He turned to Margaret who was standing in the doorway. She smiled and took the letters from his hands. She, too, was happy that her younger sons were about to become fathers and she would once more be a grandmother.

"I hope the young cousins will meet some day. The strands that tie our family will always remain strong, I am sure."

The family had settled well into the big house down on the waterfront. With Donald working in the attached shed, there was always someone on hand to help look after the shop. On fine days the handcrafts flowed out onto outdoor tables and the colourful displays attracted passersby who were often tempted to buy.

Just then, Chirsty appeared on the doorstep with baby Donald. He smiled when he saw Archibald and Margaret and held out his arms to be taken.

"He is growing more bonny by the day. Let me hold him while you go out and buy the meat for tonight's stew. I hear the butcher has some tender beef just arrived from Morven."

Chirsty was only too happy to be relieved of the child and was soon on her way to the butcher's store. She chatted to some friends beside the town clock and walked slowly past the market stalls where she picked out some fresh vegetables to go with the stew.

The move from the upper village had its advantages as everything they needed was close at hand. The children would be home from school at any time but she knew that her mother was there to care for them.

How fortunate she was to have such great support. The letter from Catherine had hinted at a busy life, and with Neil working on the new road each day, she would receive very little help with her large family.

The news of Sally's pregnancy had been read with great excitement, but would they ever see the expected child? Chirsty knew what it would have meant to old Archibald to see the first child to carry his name, although Hugh and Mary would most likely take that honour. But now it was time to stop day dreaming and return home to where the busy household awaited her.

************************

As Mary nervously awaited the birth of her first child, Hugh was working long hours out on the steep hillsides where the crafty ewes were hiding their lambs and making his job difficult.

It was time to bring the flock down to the valley for shearing and the men were busy making yards to hold the ewes and lambs. There was a great deal of commotion as lambs were separated from their mothers and Hugh was doing his best to locate every last one of them.

"There's always a few that avoid us and then they have to go many months before they can be shorn." Hugh was explaining the finer details of his job to Mary who was doing her best to show an interest.

265

She had put on a great deal of weight and was feeling very uncomfortable. She had stopped work several weeks before and spent most of the day sitting in a chair, knitting and crocheting endless little garments.

"I swear you have enough clothing for half a dozen infants. Are you sure you are only carrying one?" Hugh teased her as he tried to put his arms around her bulk.

"I'll be glad when I can see my feet again," Mary said. "No-one tells you how heavy and awkward you will get." She sighed at the thought of four more weeks before she would feel human again.

"Come along. Let's go to the tavern and have a meal there. I'm sure you would like to catch up with your friends." Hugh didn't like seeing Mary in such low spirits.

Mary brightened at the thought of talking to Annie and picked up her shawl and struggled into her shoes.

The tavern was crowded but the landlord soon found a table for Hugh and Mary and brought them a welcome tankard of ale. They were joined by several of Mary's old workmates and soon they were catching up on all the latest news.

Several of the sheep herders were also drinking in the tavern and were curious to know how Hugh's brother was progressing in New Zealand.

266

"How is that brother of yours? Is he living on his own property yet?"

Hugh was happy to share the news that Alexander and Sally had planted a crop on their land and were working for a generous landowner. "They are hoping to start building their house soon as Sally is with child. It is winter time there and they have had snow and sleet I am told."

Most of the men were surprised at that. They imagined New Zealand as some sort of tropical island where snow would have been impossible.

"They should feel right at home then. It must be very much like living right here on Mull."

Hugh agreed, but secretly thought there was no way he would ever afford his own land in Scotland. The dream of following his brother to the new country still persisted. "It would be grand to own your own acreage and build a house from timber grown on the property."

Luckily Mary wasn't close enough to hear these words as she chatted to her friend Annie.  She thought that Hugh had forgotten this unsettling dream.

Annie was thrilled that she was at long last pregnant. "I was beginning to give up hope," she laughed. "Now I suppose there will be a child every couple of years. My Robbie is thrilled as well and is busy adding a new room onto our cottage."


267

The meal was served and Hugh sat beside Mary, pleased to see that she was enjoying her evening out. "We will have to do this more often. It is good to see you so cheerful."

Mary smiled. "I didn't realise how much I have missed the company. Once the baby comes along I will be busy so it is good to make the most of the free time we have left."


********************


As the spring weather warmed the countryside, Alexander and Sally spent many hours cultivating their land and tending the crops of corn and wheat that had struggled through the winter.

With sunny days and longer evenings, Alexander was able to build a fence from sturdy posts and saplings. He had learned to shape the end of each rail so it fitted into a groove on the post and soon he had a sizeable field enclosed.

They planted grass seed and watched as the green shoots broke through the earth. "We will buy a cow and two sheep next time we are in Milton," Alexander decided and Sally was very excited when the animals were safely delivered. The cow was a large Holstein and was due to calve at any time, then Sally would be able to milk her and make their own butter.

The ewes would lamb in about a month and they hoped there would be sufficient grass to feed them all. Alexander had also bought half a dozen fine hens and had made a simple shed to house them. Sally let them wander during the day then fed them and shut them in the pen at night.

With their own milk and eggs and vegetables growing in the garden, they would soon be almost self sufficient and Alexander had never been so content.

"It would be great if Neil and Catherine could spend more time on their property. They have scarcely seen it over the winter months." Alexander was concerned at the lack of progress. The McDougall land was still in its original state with bush and scrub growing where crops and grass could have been planted.

"We will probably see more of them once summer is here. The days will be longer and they might have more time to spend on their land." Sally missed the company of Catherine and the children and hoped she would see them more once her baby was born.

With the child due in two months, she was still able to carry out some of her chores but was no longer working on Mr Green's farm. One of the worker's wives had taught her to knit and she was struggling with small squares to sew into a blanket for the baby's crib.

"We can get a ride into town on Sunday and catch up with Neil and Catherine. They are sure to be around and it will be good to see how the children are faring in their school." Alexander was keen to see Neil as he had the thought that his employer might be interested in using his land. If it could be ploughed and planted with wheat it would be easier for Neil to cultivate when the right time came.

James Green had already built a flour mill in the nearby town and was keen to encourage wheat growing to supply the mill. The more he thought about it, the more excited Alexander became.

Sally was excited too as she would enjoy the visit to town and the chance to catch up with her sister-in-law and the children. "There may have been mail from home. I often wonder how my family and old Archibald and Margaret are coping. They should know about our baby by now and I am curious as to whether Mary and Hugh are expecting a child as well."

It took many months for answers to come back from Scotland which was the most frustrating part of being so far from home and Sally was impatient to hear the latest family news from across the sea.

# Chapter 39

Winter had come to Tobermory and the children complained about the long trek up the back brae to the school. Once they arrived, the classrooms were warm and welcoming with a fire lit in the small stoves in the corner.

They warmed their hands before sitting at their desks to copy their letters and add up the numbers on the board. Soon it would be time for a hot drink and a chance to practise their music for the end of year show. There would be no visiting schools this year but their teacher was happy with the progress his pupils were making.

"Your parents will be very proud," he said. "And we will be sorry that some of our best pupils are leaving us."

Kettie blushed as he looked in her direction. She would be pleased to start work as school had little more to offer her. Her mother had found her a job in the town's bakery and she would start there at the end of the term.

She was still seeing Charles as often as she could but knew that the longer hours of work would mean less time for them to share. Charles had already started helping his father in the butcher's store which Kettie knew was not his first choice.

"I know you would rather be working on the land, but you will be able to make a living in the meantime," she said. "At least I'm not going to be helping in the house all day. I really thought my mother would expect me to do that but having her parents living with us has changed everything. Old Margaret is so capable and Archibald does a few chores from time to time."

"The butcher's shop isn't too bad. I get to do the deliveries so that can be quite interesting." Charles was settling into the work better than he thought he would and quite enjoyed driving the horse and cart around the village as he made deliveries.

They were standing under a roof down near the pier, sheltering from the cold wind that blew in from the sea. Kettie snuggled against Charles to keep warm and he responded by cradling her in his arms.

"I'm going to ask your father's permission to walk out with you. What do you say to that?"

"I'm sure he won't object. I will invite you around for tea on Sunday night and you can get to know my family better. That will be grand." Kettie was thrilled that Charles wanted their friendship to progress. Her heart beat a little faster. Life was becoming very exciting with a new job and a steady boyfriend. She was only too happy to leave her schooldays behind her.

*********************

With the chilling wind and long, dark nights, Archibald's health was suffering. He had developed a bad cough and Margaret was worried that it might turn into pneumonia if she couldn't keep him warm.

"What else can I do for him?" she asked Dr MacColl. "He is becoming so frail."

"You can't do more than you are already doing. Old Archibald is reaching the end of his days." The doctor looked sad. He had known the family for many years and had seen them come through good times and bad. "At least he will be able to see his new grandchild in a few weeks. He will happy if it is a boy to carry on the McDonald name."

"I don't think young Mary would mind what the baby is. She is very fed up with her condition right now." Margaret sighed as she thought of Hugh's wife who was not handling her pregnancy well.

"She will forget all that once she holds her child. I'm sure Hugh's wife will make a great mother." The doctor reassured Margaret. "Now, you try to get some rest and carry on the good work of looking after your husband."

273

Chirsty was anxious to hear what the doctor had to say and knew she would have to give her mother more help with nursing Archibald. "We will both look after him and I'm sure his health will improve," she said, but secretly she did not think her father was long for this world.

Archibald was soon up and about again and was able to sit in his chair by the door of the shop and talk to the people who came by. But many of his friends from Ulva had already passed on and it was almost as if he was waiting for his time to come.

Chirsty sat by his side when her mother was busy elsewhere and Archibald talked often of the good old days on the small island. She secretly thought life was much easier now that they were living in Tobermory, but her father had lived and worked with the sights and sounds of Ulva as his life blood, and the old ways were deeply engrained on his soul.

The doctor visited once in a while but knew he could do little. "Archibald's heart is getting weaker and I fear a chill could take him at any time. Keep him warm and comfortable and call me if he worsens."

Old Archibald began to spend more time resting in his bed and the family made sure that he was never alone. It was his son-in-law Donald who was at his side when the end finally came. He had listened to the laboured breathing and when the sound stopped he rose from the chair and leaned over the man lying silent on the bed.

"Farewell old Archibald," he whispered gently as he pulled the blanket over his face. "You have led a good life and left strong seed behind. God bless you on your final journey."

Archibald McDonald was the first of the family to be laid to rest in the grave yard on the hillside of Tobermory. It seemed that even in death he was not destined to return to the island of Ulva where his ancestors had been buried in ancient cemeteries.

"We want to be close to our father's grave," Chirsty insisted and Margaret was too overwhelmed with grief to argue. Yes. It would be comforting to know that her husband lay close by and she could walk up the Back Brae to visit his burial place.

She lived through the week following Archibald's death in a daze. Although she had been prepared for the inevitable, when the time came it left her feeling numb and disconnected, as though the life blood had been drained out of her.

"Alexander and Catherine don't know about their father. It will be many weeks before the news reaches them," she lamented. She had mailed a letter to New Zealand a few days after the burial but the boat would take several months to get there.

275

"You will have two new grandchildren before you know it," Chirsty said. "I think it is time you visited Hugh and Mary in Salen so you can be there when the child comes."

Margaret wasn't keen to leave so soon after her husband's death but knew that young Mary would appreciate the help so she quietly packed a bag and was ready for the mail cart the next morning.

When she was dropped off outside the post office she looked around her. The street was busy as she walked towards Hugh's cottage and when she arrived she was in for a big surprise. The doctor was just coming out through the front door followed by her son who had a big smile on his face.

"Mary has just given birth to a bonny girl. They are both fine although she is very tired." He led his mother into the bedroom where Mary lay, holding a small bundle in her arms.

"You couldn't have come at a better time. I don't know the first thing about looking after a child." Margaret smiled and took the baby in her arms, holding her close. Mary sighed and closed her eyes, turning away from the light.

"It is good for you to rest and I will care for the child in the meantime." Margaret laid the baby in the wooden cradle and rocked it gently. The little girl looked around for a moment then closed her eyes and went to sleep.

276

"We will let your wife and daughter catch up on some sleep. In the meantime I'll fix us a drink and you can tell me all about the birth."

Hugh couldn't go into too much detail as he had left Mary in the doctor's care and only returned when he was told the good news. "She was feeling restless in the night and I called the doctor when the pains got bad. I didn't want to get in the way so I left them to it."

It sounded like a typical male reaction and Margaret handed him a mug of tea and poured one for herself. She could see that she had arrived just at the right time and there would be plenty for her to do.

"I will stay and help Mary for as long as she needs me. It will take my mind off your father's passing."

Hugh looked gratefully across at his mother. He had attended the funeral and returned home straight afterwards. There had been no time to talk of his father and share their grief.

"Thank you, and we've decided that the baby will carry your name. Margaret Ann, for you and Mary's mother. We will be glad if you can stay until Mary is back on her feet as I really should be out with the flock at such a busy time."

Hugh finished his tea and crept in to check on his wife. She lay peacefully asleep but the baby was beginning to stir. Her eyes opened and she began to wail. Margaret soon gathered her up and wrapped her more firmly. "We will give Mary a drink and then she must feed the child."

A short time later, Mary had been wakened and she sat in the bed awkwardly holding the baby to her breast. After a time the child began to suck and Hugh looked on in delight, as Margaret left them together to enjoy their new daughter.

# Chapter 40

Catherine was taken by surprise as her brother walked up the path and knocked on the front door. She had not seen him for several weeks and threw her arms around his tall, lean frame.

"It's so good to see someone from my old life once in a while. I am making many new friends but there is nothing better than catching up with family."

She was surprised to see Sally in such an advanced state of pregnancy. "Come in and rest after your long ride. I'm sure that being bounced around on a cart is not at all comfortable."

Sally agreed as she lowered herself into a chair and placed her feet on a low stool. "I must admit I will be happy when the baby arrives. It is getting most difficult to carry out my chores the way I am."

They chatted for a while until Neil and the children arrived, each carrying a load of firewood. They threw it onto the pile by the back door and washed their hands in the bucket outside.

Archibald had news for Neil about his allotment. James Green was willing to lease the land and plant a crop of wheat and the news was received with great excitement. "We were anxious that nothing was being done to the land. At least that will carry us over until we can move there and start using it ourselves."

Sally was pleased to catch up with the children and was anxious to hear all about their activities. She felt very proud when she heard about young Sarah's success at the concert.

"I'm sure you will be very famous one day and everyone will be talking about you," she said, much to Sarah's embarrassment.

Alexander was amazed at the improvements Neil had made to the cottage. It was looking very homely with new shelving and cupboards, as well as a sturdy table and new stools. "I want to begin building our own dwelling but there don't seem to be enough hours in the day," he admitted. "In the meantime we are quite comfortable in Mr Green's cottage."

As they left later in the day, it was decided that Sally should return the following week and stay with Catherine until after the baby was born. It was unlikely that the midwife would travel all the way to their farm and she would have more help if she stayed in Milton.

Alexander was relieved at the news and they agreed that Sally would return in a few days' time. They borrowed the horse and cart for the return journey, promising to return it soon. "We can test out our new fences and see whether it will keep the horse from wandering," he laughed as they drove away.

"We should be able to buy our own horse and buggy soon. It is difficult to be sharing with my brother-in-law. We will need to fence off some more pasture though as a horse eats far more than the sheep and cow."

They made plans as they jogged along the rough track towards their rented cottage, feeling positive about their future.

*********************

A whole month went by before Margaret felt confident about leaving Mary and Hugh to fend for themselves. The baby was thriving but seemed to need constant attention and Mary was struggling to cope. "I just seem to finish feeding her and she is hungry again," she complained.

Margaret solved the problem by feeding the baby some thin porridge from a spoon which she sucked hungrily. "She is such a little pig," she laughed as she poured another spoonful into the baby's mouth. "But she is a big child and needs something more than milk."

Mary was relieved when little Margaret finally fell asleep. "I'm so glad that you have been able to stay and help me. I don't think I could have handled it by myself."

Margaret knew that she needed to return home and let Mary run her own household. The longer she stayed, the more the younger woman was relying on her. Besides, she was looking forward to getting back to Tobermory and helping out at the craft shop. She needed to weave a blanket for her new grand-daughter and another to mail to Sally ready for her infant.

Chirsty was pleased to see her mother looking so cheerful when she alighted from the mail cart. She laughed when she heard about Mary struggling to manage one small child. "Heaven help her if she has a brood like mine."

There was great excitement as they shared the news of the new baby and when they visited the shop, Margaret was surprised at the number of items which had been sold in her absence. She would need to get around to their suppliers and bring in more stock to fill the shelves.

It was almost dark when she found the time to climb the steep road up to the grave yard. The flowers had wilted and a white cross had been installed to mark the plot. She stood in silence, looking over the mound of earth and out towards the sea where the shape of the distant islands could be seen.

"Goodbye my beloved, until we meet again. You will never be far from my thoughts."

She picked a handful of flowers and placed them in a container which had held a few withered plants, then walked back down to the village to her new life.



Once Alexander and Sally had returned to their allotment they let the horse go in the field along with the cow and sheep. He raced around for a moment and then stood, contently eating the rich green grass. There was no way he was going anywhere.

They returned to their cottage where Sally fell into bed, exhausted from her long day. "I will miss you so much if I go to stay with Catherine and Alexander, but at least I will have company when the baby comes."

Over the next few days, Sally fed the hens and tidied the cottage. A wooden cradle was ready for the new child and she packed a number of small garments along with the clothes she would need to take over to Milton.

Alexander took the day off work to drive the horse and cart back to the village. He would walk back later in the day as he wanted to spend some time working on the new fence. An area of land had been ploughed and was ready for more grass seed to be planted. By the time Sally returned with their child the new calf and lambs should be born and they would soon need the extra grazing land.

They drove over the rough track at a slow pace and took in the vista of hills and bush, interspersed with grassy fields. A number of small dwellings were beginning to appear as the settlers moved their families on to their allotments. Spirals of smoke rose from the cooking stoves and children could be seen playing in the sunshine.

"I want to begin building our own house as soon as possible," Alexander said, as he looked at Sally with pride. "We will need a proper place to bring up our child. A place he can call his home."

Sally placed her hand on her extended stomach. "It may be a little girl you know. But you are right. We will start on the house as soon as I return from Milton."

# Chapter 41

After a short, exhausting labour, Archibald John McDonald came into the world, red faced and crying. Sally closed her eyes in relief as Catherine and the midwife cleaned the child and wrapped him in a cosy blanket. "Here you are, my dear. Take your little boy who is a fine, healthy child."

Sally held her arms out to take her son and wished fervently that her husband was there to share the precious moment. As soon as Sally had gone into labour, Neil had ridden off to tell Alexander the news, but the baby had been born before they returned.

"He will be here soon, I am sure," Catherine placated her. "And he will be so proud of you and your new son."

The children had been banished from the house and now they came trooping back and stood shyly in the doorway, eager to meet their new cousin. "Why is his face so red?" The little boys were curious. The girls gazed in wonder at the little infant lying in his mother's arms.

Just at that moment, there was the sound of horse's hooves on the gravel road and Sally pulled herself up and looked out the window.

"Alexander and Neil have arrived." Her face was radiant as Alexander walked into the room and stared in disbelief at his beautiful little boy.

He threw his arms around Sally and gave her a sound kiss. "Well done, my darling. You have given me a precious son."

Catherine bustled around, sending the children out of the room to give the new parents some privacy. She realized that it was past dinner time and with the help of the older girls, set about preparing a meal. "We must feed the men folk and I am sure Sally will be ready for something tasty," she said. "Alexander will stay here for the night so you boys can bed down together."

The children rushed off to arrange the mattresses, excited that their uncle would be spending the night with them.

Alexander was reluctant to leave his wife's side but was enticed by the delicious aroma coming from the kitchen. "If only we could let our parents know that they have a new grandson and his name is Archibald. It will be many weeks before they hear the good news."

He looked out at the full moon high in the sky and knew that the people back in Scotland would see the same moon that night. The strands across the sea would never be broken.

✱✱✱✱✱✱✱✱✱✱✱✱✱✱✱✱✱✱✱✱✱✱

A week went by before Sally was ready to accompany Alexander back to the small cottage on James Green's property. The summer sun was warming the earth and the crops were springing up, ready to be harvested.

As they drove past their own property Sally was delighted to see a new calf suckling his mother and two tiny lambs chasing each other around the field. "What a surprise. You didn't tell me about the new arrivals."

"I thought it would be a nice welcome home present for you my dear. But it means that you will be kept busy milking the cow and making the butter."

Sally smiled. She knew that the calf would take most of the milk but there could well be enough for them to share.

Alexander had begun fencing another large paddock ready for the horse they hoped to buy. Sharing the horse and buggy with Neil and Catherine was no longer practical and although Alexander knew he could borrow a mount from his employer, they needed their own transport.

But the biggest surprise came when Sally looked up the hill and realized that her husband had been busy working on the house site. A simple frame had been erected and a few planks were already in place to form the walls.

287

"Mr Green gave me time off so I could work on the house. Enough boards have been milled to cover the frame and although the interior will have to wait, we should be able to move in quite soon. One day it will be a fine home for our little son."

They drove a little further until they reached the crude little cottage, then Alexander carried the small child inside and laid him in the wooden cradle with the soft woven blankets that old Margaret had woven. "Your grandmother would be very happy to see you," he said tenderly. He turned to Sally and held her tightly. "I will write to tell them of little Archibald's safe arrival. Let's hope that my father is still well enough to enjoy the good news."

**********************

The village of Tobermory was humming with activity. Spring was in the air and the gardens were a riot of colour and fragrant with blossom. Chirsty had persuaded many of the shopkeepers to plant barrels of bright flowers outside their premises and these were much admired by the visitors who flocked to the town from the mainland.

Old Margaret had arranged for a number of women to supply handcrafted goods and the store was bright with colourful scarves, shawls and

288

rugs, as well as carved wooden toys and ornaments made by the men.

As Margaret checked the items on the long table outside the shop, Maggie Black came into view waving a bundle of letters. "I couldn't wait. I had to bring you this mail which just arrived this morning. I know you are most anxious to get news of your family so far away."

Margaret thanked the woman and rushed into the store, clutching the precious packages to her breast. "Chirsty, Donald, come and look. We have mail from New Zealand."

Donald stopped what he was doing and came over to share the excitement. Chirsty laid little Donald down on a rug and sat beside her mother as they spread the letters out on the table. "They have all written. Where should we start?" Margaret picked up the letter from her son and ripped it open.

Her eyes filled with tears as she read the welcome news. "Another Archibald has been born," she sobbed. "And they don't yet know that old Archibald has gone."

Chirsty took the letter from her mother and read out the words. "We are very happy to tell you of the safe arrival of little Archibald John McDonald. Sally is very well and the bairn is thriving." She read the rest of the letter which painted a vivid picture of their busy life in the new land.

The next package was from Catherine and included notes from the children, who shared news of their activities. "Father has made our cottage very comfortable and we are happy that we have our own cat and five kittens."

"School is alright most of the time but the big girls are bossy and make us do our sums and reading when we get home at night."

"I sang in the school concert and there is a music teacher in Milton who is coaching me free of charge."

"Our Aunt Sally had a new baby right in our house but we weren't allowed to watch. At first he had a red face and has lots of black hair."

Margaret laughed as she read the messages. She could imagine the children sitting at the table struggling to write down their news.

Catherine's letter was more serious. There was a delay in moving to their own land, but life in Milton was busy. They had made many friends and there were plenty of activities for herself and the children. Neil was still working on the new road and their allotment was being leased to grow wheat. "I think it will be some time before we can move the children out to our land as they are very settled in the school here and we have made our cottage very comfortable."

"It seems that New Zealand is suiting the family well." Donald said, as he returned to his work. He often wondered how life would have turned out for his family if they had made the long journey. He looked across at his wife sharing the news with her mother. They sat close together as they read of the families so far away.

He knew that the strands across the sea were as strong as ever.